Being Elsewhere

by

John P. Sisk

EWU
Eastern Washington University Press
Cheney, Washington

AC
8
S 556
1994

Being Elsewhere
First Edition, October, 1994

Eastern Washington University Press
Mail Stop 133, Showalter Hall
Eastern Washington University
Cheney, WA 99004-2431

ISBN   0-910055-15-7 Paperback
        0-910055-16-5 Hardback

        Library of Congress Cataloging-in-Publication Data

Sisk, John P., 1914–
    Being elsewhere / John P. Sisk. — 1st ed.
        p. cm.
    ISBN 0-910055-16-5 : $25.00. — ISBN 0-910055-15-7 (pbk.) : $12.50
    I. Title
    AC8.S556   1994
    081–dc20   94-29354
                                                            CIP

For My Children

Also by John P. Sisk

Person and Institution (1970)
The Tyrannies of Virtue (1990)

Contents

$\mathcal{F}$*oreword*

The first elsewhere we encounter is the buzzing confusion of the world into which we are born, at which point we become dependent on continuing encounters with elsewheres for information about the new environment. Early on we learn to avoid unpromising elsewheres, often on the basis of inadequate or biased information, and often, too, out of a sense that the comfortable place we inhabit might be destroyed by the new information. It's not easy to forget the sad experience of Adam and Eve. Persuaded by the Prince of all travel agents that a better environment was available to them, they lost the one they had and were forced to set out on their travels knowing that the Great Good Place was behind them. They were the first to learn one of the risks of encountering elsewheres: you may only discover how foolish you were to leave home.

There is no reason to believe that Adam and Eve were bored in the Garden of Eden. Nevertheless, boredom with the daily routine is a strong motivation for travel—one that combines easily with the expectation that an encounter with the Great Good Place, out there somewhere, will glorify existence. You meet bored but still wistful travelers everywhere. A few fortunate ones, having adjusted their expectations, now see themselves and their world in a new context and so have ceased to be bored, just as they have ceased to be disillusioned when elsewheres prove to be only themselves and not Great Good Places.

But if the yearning for the Great Good Place impels many people to unlikely elsewheres, it can also be exploited to keep other people at home. Thus countries of the Marxist persuasion, who not so long ago advertised themselves as the Great Good Places of the heart's desire, wisely prevented their inmates from traveling to alien elsewheres where fresh information might disillusion them. So Marxism, whatever it was in theory, was in practice no friend of the travel industry. After all, it promised a world in which everyone, happy to be where they were, would not dream of being anywhere else.

Still, and paradoxically, there are few elsewheres in which one cannot meet "fellow travelers" who judge all places against the socialist dream of the Great Good Place. They are like those servicemen whose experiences of exotic elsewheres in World War II were too filtered through, and buffered by, images and habits of home to be truly educational. Now some of their children, having discovered virtual reality by way of cocaine and the machinery of hypermedia, are learning how easy it is to encounter fabulous elsewheres without leaving home at all.

Of course, the primary aim of the service's various branches was to overcome the enemy, not to prepare its members to be more humanely at large in a peacetime world about which they had acquired a good deal of firsthand information. Nevertheless, the latter is what could and often did happen. This is why William James, himself an avid traveler, believed that if civilization is to survive, it needs a moral equivalent of war. Ultimately, this is to believe that there is a close connection between the welfare of the human race and its freedom to travel in the interest of being more enrichingly at home in the world.

Trouble and Travel
1985

t is common knowledge that certain vocal minorities in Europe would prefer that Americans go home and stay home. For such people the future looks bleak indeed. In 1984 they had to find a way to live with five and a half million American invaders, a figure that is expected to increase in 1985 since the British pound, French franc, West German mark, and Italian lira continue to lose ground against the American dollar. The likely thing, of course, is that most of these millions will think of themselves as well-disposed visitors, not invaders: what foreigner with something to sell or rent could be anything but ecstatically happy at the prospect of more American dollars? The likely thing too is that most of the visitor-invaders will set out with the golden expectations that the travel industry encourages, paying no more attention to *Time's* timely warning that all travel in foreign countries "is a matter of cumulative exposure to the unknown and unpredictable" than picnic-bound children do to parental reminders about the threat of bumblebee stings and poison ivy.

Nevertheless, all travel, including the elaborately planned and technologically controlled travel of astronauts, can be defined as a movement between a familiar and less familiar place in the process of which things normally go wrong. Though most of us know this as a fact of past experience, we keep anticipating the trouble-free trip, probably for the same reason we keep buying tickets in state lotteries and drinking martinis before dinner: the alternative is unthinkable. So we change travel agencies, update our checklists in the light of past oversights, consult the stars before setting departure dates, increase our portfolio of credit cards, avoid unreliable airlines and flights that are destined to deposit us after dark in strange airports, commit our Michelins to memory, take crash courses in French, German, Italian, or Spanish. Still, as my wife and I discovered long ago, things keep going wrong.

Those traveler-invaders who find intolerable the contretemps that are to be expected in any passage from a familiar to an unfamiliar place may be happy to learn that there are systems that reduce, if not entirely eliminate, the number of things that can go wrong. In his excellent book *Life in the English Country House*, Mark Girouard describes the system of the medieval traveling household. As they moved from castle to castle, the Lord and his Lady simply took their home environment with them—not only their scores, even hundreds of retainers, but "plate, jewels, tapestries, table-cloths, clothing, hangings, coffers, musical instruments, carpenter's tools, mass-books, mass-vessels, vestments, linen, pots and pans, cooking-pits, and beds by the dozen." Like Ringling Brothers on the move, such a traveling household even had its advance agents whose jobs it was to make sure that the household's destination was ready to receive it and that nothing would go wrong upon arrival.

Then there is the method demonstrated by Des Esseintes, the decadent central figure of J. K. Huysmans's late nineteenth century French novel, *Against the Grain*. Suddenly possessed by a desire to go to England, he has himself and his luggage transported to the neighborhood of a Paris railroad station with sufficient time to visit a bistro and a restaurant, in both of which the presence of English-speaking people evokes sensations of London he has acquired from the novels of Dickens. Aware then that in the actual journey he will only "lose those imperishable sensations" as reality fails once more to measure up to anticipation, he does not board the train for Dieppe but returns with his luggage to his home in Fortenay, "feeling the physical stimulation and the moral fatigue of a man coming back to his home after a long and dangerous voyage." This may be an extreme of sentimentalism, but insofar as travel is a state of mind (and it is at least that) here is a foolproof way to keep things from going wrong.

And there is Thoreau's superficially similar system. In an age when his contemporaries were going off in all directions, Thoreau, one of whose overriding concerns was to keep himself from being invaded, was able to say with some complacency: "I have traveled a good deal in Concord." He had indeed. In *Thoreau As World Traveler* John Aldrich Christie takes twenty pages to list the travel literature that Thoreau obviously read with fascinated attention and referred to in his *Journal* and other writings. Despite the fact that "by want of pecuniary wealth, I have been nailed down to this my native region so long and so steadily," he came to know

North America, Asia, and Africa in great detail while avoiding the inconveniences that even the most fortunate travelers must expect. For this kind of traveler the worst thing that can go wrong is not to be able to get the book you want when you want it.

There are reasons to believe that Thoreau would have been an unhappy traveler even if he had not wanted pecuniary wealth. Unlike his traveling friends, Emerson and Hawthorne, he did not like cities. "Who can see these cities and say there is any life in them?" he wrote while visiting New York. Things went wrong for him in cities. Besides, for a traveler he had a disastrous attachment to freedom: "I must not lose any of my freedom by being a farmer and landholder. Most who enter on any profession are doomed men," he wrote in his *Journal*. Imagine him, like Emerson on *his* first trip abroad, cramped into a small cabin with four seasick strangers for six storm-tossed weeks followed by two weeks of quarantine in the harbor at Malta. For that matter, imagine a man of "such dangerous frankness," as Emerson said of Thoreau, confined for eight or ten hours in a 747, or stalled for ten minutes between stations in a London underground train. Such a man had better do his traveling in Concord.

But at least Thoreau was by temperament kept from making the mistake so many travelers make when they assume that "travel" and "freedom" are synonyms. A familiar ad for a seven-day Caribbean cruise exploits this assumption: in a world of bougainvillea blossoms, tropical drinks, and sugar-white beaches you will feel "gloriously, unselfconsciously free." By implication those who are free travel, those who aren't stay home—except that the reverse is sometimes just as true. It is probably better for the traveler not to anticipate states of liberation so that when they happen they can be appreciated like unanticipated favorable changes in currency exchange. The sober fact is that once you have made hotel reservations, bought airline tickets and the necessary new clothes, farmed out the dog, arranged to have the mail collected and the premises looked after, you are no longer free to stay home.

Paul Fussell in "The Stationary Tourist" (*Harper's*, April 1979) makes a useful distinction between exploration (the Renaissance), travel (the bourgeois age), and tourism (the proletarian present). In this progression things are less likely to go wrong as you approach the tourist present. But this is purely academic information to a tourist confined, as we once were, to a couchette with five other people in an Italian railroad car without water and flushable toilets. Such a person will take little comfort from the thought that things must often have been worse for Darwin on the *Beagle*, or that the most miserable Italian train offers a king's luxury compared with the primitive transportation available to Goethe in his late eighteenth-century tour of Italy.

Speaking relatively, then, probably more things go wrong for tourists than for explorers or travelers, in spite of the assistance of travel bureaus, tour guides, the sophistications of communication and transportation, and the general availability of basic creature comforts. If in September of 1519 you had set out with Magellan in search of a westward route to the Spice Islands, you would have expected to rough it. If in early 1833 you had traveled with Emerson from Malta to London, you probably would not have been demoralized by a twenty-four hour storm-tossed crossing of the English Channel. But now when all factors involved (including one's own pampered utopian impulses) combine to induce expectations of comfortable trouble-free touring, an air-controllers' strike at Heathrow or a missed connection at O'Hare can be psychologically as devastating as the mutiny Magellan had to contend with at Port San Julian.

Indeed, the modern expectation of liberated trouble-free travel has such a built-in potential for frustration that tourism for many people is the repeated experience of the great theme of literary modernism: the discovery of illusion. This means that the would-be tourist had better learn to read the travel sections of the popular magazines and Sunday papers with an ironic eye; otherwise he is likely to believe that a sortie over Spain in a hot air balloon or a photographic safari in the wilds of Botswana will be as safe and comfortable as a jog in the park. Such expectations prepare for the disillusionment that led Mark Twain to write in his notebook after seeing the Taj Mahal: "God will be a disappointment to most of us." And of all things that go wrong when one travels, disillusionment is one of the most painful.

Ironic travelers have usually learned early not only that it is pointless to expect that nothing will go wrong but that things must go wrong if travel is to be interesting. The good trip is the one that makes a good story, and good stories depend on the right kind of troubles, which make possible memorable reversals of expectation and serendipitous events. This is as true of "Love Boat" as of *Gulliver's Travels*. If Darwin's five-year tour on the *Beagle* had turned out to be the story he expected, the tour would have been long ago forgotten. But if ironic travelers know that what they go for is often different or less than they come home with, they also know that what they get when things go wrong is not necessarily any better than what they might have gotten if everything had gone according to plan. What goes wrong eliminates, for better or worse, one possible future while it actualizes another.

Fussell speaks of those anti-tourists who attempt to prove themselves travelers, or even explorers, by making a point of keeping off the beaten track and avoiding standard points of interest. For them St. Peters, the Eiffel Tower, Disneyland, Westminster Abbey, the Grand Canyon, the Berlin Wall, Ponte Vecchio, and the Great Pyramid at Gizeh are places not to see, or to be carefully censored out of one's conversation afterwards if they cannot be avoided. Anti-tourists wouldn't be caught dead in a tour group unless, perhaps, it was headed for penguin-watching at the Antarctic ice barrier or whale-watching in the Sea of Cortes. Unfortunately, the very nature of such off-beat excursions makes them overprotective and therefore reduces the margin for adventure and reminiscence. Besides, anti-tourists may be making the same tactical mistake that the philosopher of science Thomas S. Kuhn believes many aspiring scientists make when, in their passion for the dramatic innovations that bring Nobel prizes, they forget that the important innovators now "work within a well-defined and deeply ingrained tradition." Transpose this paradox into travel language, and it suggests that there may be a better chance for things to go interestingly and memorably wrong if one stays on the beaten paths.

Tourists, travelers, and explorers have one thing in common: direction. No matter how much goes wrong or what changes of itinerary become necessary, all three expect to return to the point from which they started. Thus their peregrinations have what Aristotle expected to see in good drama: a beginning, a middle, and an end. But there is another category of traveler (if I may return to the more familiar sense of the term) and this is the wanderer. The classic wanderer is Ulysses, not the hero of Homer's epic but the figure we meet in canto 26 of Dante's *Inferno* and later in Tennyson's dramatic monologue "Ulysses." This latter Ulysses, like many war veterans, has found home a bore and determines to set out with congenial companions "To sail beyond the sunset, and the baths/Of all the western stars, until I die." He probably would agree with T. S. Eliot's remark in "East Coker" that "Old men ought to be explorers," but he is not really an explorer. An explorer aims to return to the human community with useful information, and this is not what Ulysses has in mind. If he has any use for us it is thanks to the poet who enshrines him as a model of geriatric derring-do. He needs no itinerary, no travel agent, no reservations; everything he owns, we must assume, will go under the seat in front of him. Nothing can go wrong since all eventualities are equally acceptable—short of that unlikely one that would redirect him back home to his aged Penelope.

Coleridge's Ancient Mariner, too, is a wanderer, and so are Byron, Shelley, D. H. Lawrence, Hemingway, and F. Scott Fitzgerald. There is something about romantic personalities, creatures of process and becoming as they are, that inclines them to keep on going once they leave their point of origin. We have seen bedraggled late-twentieth-century versions of them everywhere in Europe: strumming their guitars for small change in Paris Métro tunnels or spaced out on the Ponte Vecchio in Florence or on the Spanish Steps in Rome. They have to be distinguished, no doubt, from the youngsters who are simply taking an inexpensive Grand Tour, but most of them, we suspected, were the lost children of the world who neither had nor any longer wanted direction, for whom things had gone wrong for so long that living with wrongness had become a way of life.

Thoreau, the stationary world traveler, had it right when he wrote in his *Journal:* "Only that traveling is good which reveals to me the value of home and enables me to enjoy it better." Travel doesn't so much free us from home as make us freer at home. "Traveling is a fool's paradise," Emerson wrote in "Self-Reliance," but in order to know this he had to travel widely and with considerable gusto, as he would continue to do after he wrote it, travel being for him, as for most of us, an act of self-definition. Whether we explore, travel, or tour, we submit ourselves to the vicissitudes of the world in order to define home in more expansive terms, just as we submit ourselves to wilderness in order to define civilization in more expansive terms. But if we stay home out of fear that things will go wrong, home becomes increasingly more confining. And this means that things have gone very wrong indeed.

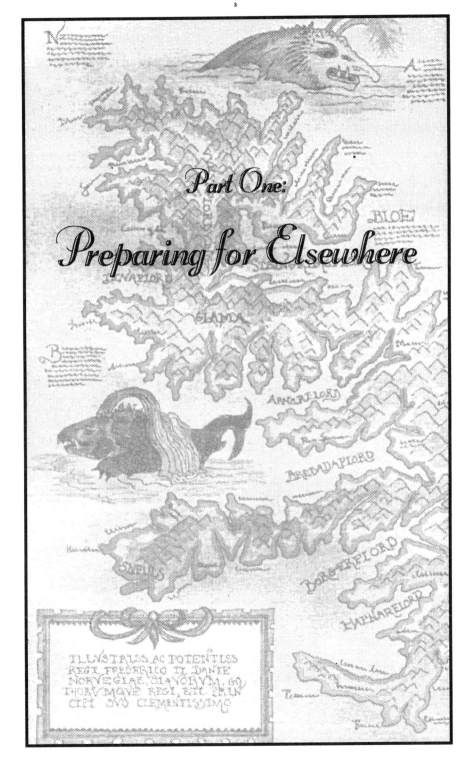

Part One:

Preparing for Elsewhere

Rising In The World
1922 - 1936

ike many another, I entered the labor force carrying things. For two grade-school years in the early 1920s I carried the *Pictorial Review* around my lower-middle-class neighborhood, and for the subsequent ten years I carried golf clubs around the local Country Club. I began each job with the highest expectations and continued with each well beyond the point when it should have been clear that it was a dead end.

Initially the magazine job was full of golden promise. By accepting it I not only got an attractive canvas shoulder bag on which was boldly inscribed the name of the handsome magazine, but I became a functioning part of a nationwide organization called the Young Hustlers. As a Young Hustler I received a membership manual, the ethos of which was pure Horatio Alger. The manual also indicated how many magazines you would have to sell in order to be eligible for a variety of enticingly illustrated prizes. I immediately set my sights on the bicycle beside which stood a proud and happy youngster who, as it turned out, sold more copies in a month than I did in a year.

The magazines were delivered to my home each month by my agent, a neatly dressed and earnest young man who, presumably, was an example of what a Young Hustler could become if he put into practice the precepts advocated in the manual. My father thought he was a real go-getter, and the whole family was impressed with his black touring car; parked in front of the house in a neighborhood where few people owned autos, it gave us a momentary distinction.

As the manual emphasized, Young Hustlers were independent businessmen intent on rising in the world. I sold the magazine for fifteen cents a copy, four cents of which was clear profit for me. The remainder I had to keep safe until the agent returned at the end of the month to pick up the unsold copies. How much of the remaining eleven cents the agent kept himself I didn't know but I imagined that he was doing all right since, as I subsequently learned, he was agent for a crew of Young Hustlers. Each month he left me fifty magazines of which I managed to sell forty, so that at the end of the month, when I settled my affairs with him, I had to feel that once more I had let him down. Nevertheless, I was making a dollar and sixty cents a month at a time when, existentially, it was worth a great deal more. After all, a candy bar that now costs fifty cents could then be had for a nickel. Since my uncomplaining parents were supplying room, board, and clothing, I had every reason to believe that independent business was indeed the way to rise in the world.

Occasionally all the Young Hustlers in town gathered with their agents for a morale-raising banquet in a local hotel. At these affairs it was discouraging to see how many Young Hustlers were nascent hoodlums: they threw peas and pieces of hard roll at one another and looked downright cynical as a featured speaker, a super agent from regional or national headquarters, told us how to be better salesmen. The key to success, he would say, was knowing our product and believing in it. If we did not study the magazine each month we could never persuade a housewife that she could not do without it, that we were actually doing her a favor by bringing it to her door.

In the beginning, determined to be a good Young Hustler, rise in the world, and perhaps even win a bicycle, I studied the magazine conscientiously before setting out on my route. My problem, however, was that no amount of study could overcome my growing disbelief in my product. It was given over to romantic stories, recipes, illustrated patterns, and advertisements for various ointments, anointments, unguents, and creams. When a housewife said she didn't want to buy a magazine I rarely attempted to change her mind, sensing perhaps that it would be presumptuous for a mere child to aim so high. In fact, I was on her side to begin with. Thus I was acting in bad faith as I trudged about my route, living for the moment when, having sold my fortieth copy, I could hang up my bag until the next month and for a couple of weeks become the lazy and irresponsible playboy that all adolescents long to be.

From this living hell I was saved by an older grade-school friend (he was, in fact, a bit of a delinquent) who persuaded me to skip the last class one spring afternoon and hitchhike with him to the Country Club. Here the caddymaster accepted me on trial, my friend gave me a brief schooling in caddy deportment, and

I got a nine-hole job that paid me fifty cents. Soon I was caddying regularly on Saturdays, Sundays, and holidays, getting ninety cents for one bag and a dollar and twenty cents for two. For a couple of months I tried to keep the magazine route going, but by then my father was sufficiently impressed by my new independent business to agree that I had better let the old one go. The agent was obviously saddened but he wished me well as I settled my account with him for the last time and handed over my Young Hustler's bag. There was a modicum of sadness for me as well: not only was a distinctive period in my life ending but I was never going to win a bicycle. Instead, I cashed in my accumulated sales points for a Boy Scout-endorsed pocket knife.

My previous job had finally demonstrated the close connection between golden expectations and dead ends. This connection was hidden from the true-believing Young Hustler by a rhetoric that kept the emphasis on long-term and even self-transcending objectives, not on the four cents per copy profit, and never let him forget that he was part of an elite company. This meant that the Young Hustler always had on his back, along with his magazines, the burden of the future. One of the initial attractions of caddying was that it relieved me of this burden: I could quite frankly, and in good faith, live a selfish, profit-motivated and laissez faire existence. Like any lazy life, its golden promise was that it could not possibly turn out to be one more dead end. Perhaps this promise, more even than the money, gave me the sense of being away from home for the first time in my life.

Besides, there was the adventure of hitchhiking the ten or twelve miles to the course. Normally it was no problem; there was plenty of traffic going north into the agricultural suburbs and the drivers who stopped for you usually knew that your destiny was the Country Club. But it was always possible that the Good Samaritan who picked you up was turning off in another direction once he got a few miles out of town and so you were dropped off in the middle of nowhere, possibly having to walk the last four or five miles. It was not the best way to get to a job that would be all walking once you got there, but at least it was schooling for a world in which the chances are always good that you will arrive at your destination (when you don't miss it altogether) by unanticipated and not always interesting byways. This is an important lesson for anyone who hopes ultimately to travel far from home, but a Young Hustler, confined to his own neighborhood since that was where family acquaintances were most likely to buy his product, had little chance to learn it.

Of course, the caddying life left room for purely short-term ambitions—like being able to go to the movies more often, secure in the knowledge that I could afford a Coney Island hotdog afterwards and still have enough money left for carfare home. In the back of my mind too there was always the thought that I might in time earn enough money to get the bicycle I had never been able to earn in my foot-dragging days as a Young Hustler. Then the golf world had its own openings into the future. The caddymaster, his proshop assistants, and some of the groundskeepers, had all begun as caddies. Dick, the protagonist in Ring Lardner's "A Caddy's Diary," aspires to become a golf pro and golf writer as well, despite the handicap of being a semiliterate high school dropout. He bears the burden of the future as confidently as any Young Hustler. Unfortunately, being underqualified for this future (a tragic predicament of little interest to a moralist like Horatio Alger), Dick's ambitious life plan will only delay his discovery that he is a natural-born dead-ender.

I soon learned that a caddy did not have to know nearly as much as a successful Young Hustler, and that what he had to know was quickly learned: the rudimentary rules of the game, the names and functions of the golf clubs, the importance of keeping a respectful and quiet distance from your employer while he was shooting, how to mark the spot where an errant shot entered the rough so that the ball could be quickly found, how to manage the flagstick while the putting was going on, how to replace divots, etc. Besides, it was a leisurely job with plenty of restful pauses built into it, so that carrying two bags for eighteen holes in that pastoral environment was less tiring than carrying a bagful of *Pictorial Reviews* around my dismal and dog-infested route. I did not know the youngster who had inherited the route but the occasional sight of him defined my liberation.

The caddy's day began with the problem of getting to the golf course in time for the "draw"—the lottery that determined the sequence in which caddies would be called up for jobs. After this ritual we were left with a two- to three-hour interval before the golfers themselves began to arrive, filling the parking lot with vehicles that made my agent's old touring car look pretty shabby. In this free time the caddies lolled on the grass behind the eighteenth green swapping scabrous stories, carved graffiti on the walls of the caddy shack, played a chip-and-putt course they had hacked out of the wilderness behind the shack, weeded greens under supervision of the groundskeeper to earn playing privileges (nine holes for an hour's work), played touch football on a little-used section of the sixteenth fairway, or if the weather was warm enough went swimming in the little river that separated the lower reaches of the course from the rattlesnake-infested highlands beyond.

I soon found that the caddies too could be nascent hoodlums, but for the most part they were a decent lot, many of whom under less relaxed circumstances might have been successful Young Hustlers. In fact, one of my new friends had been a moderately successful *Saturday Evening Post* Young Hustler who had abandoned his route for the same reason I had abandoned mine: because of what Karl Marx called "the divine power of money." Marx himself, of course, had a Young Hustler's unshakable commitment to a golden future. In fact, to judge from the disparaging remarks that caddies in their down moods could make about the rich tightwads for whom they had to slave, there may even have been nascent Marxists among us, doomed in time to discover the dead end of another golden future.

But before my first caddying year was over there was another discovery. One beautiful spring morning a panel truck came up the service road from the lower reaches of the course and parked strangely between the first tee and the caddyhouse. Word came down to us that it contained the body of a man who had been pulled out of the river. The driver and another man were talking to the caddymaster. Curiosity seekers were obviously not welcome, but a few of us got close enough to the truck to see two muddy and heavy-booted feet lying on the open tailgate, everything else being covered with a gray blanket or tarp. The caddymaster angrily waved us away. Later, various stories circulated: the man had been murdered, he was a bootlegger who had been shot trying to escape the police, he was a fisherman who had slipped off into deep water in the little river, etc. In any event, I'd seen death for the first time, and the image of the two muddied boots stayed with me all afternoon as I worked my eighteen holes.

Inevitably, in the pursuit of money I established a relationship with a social class that had already risen in the world. The men and women I caddied for obviously had money. They could afford to belong to a private club; they dressed modishly, owned the best golf equipment, and refused to play with scuffed-up balls; they owned expensive cars. They were the makers and shakers of the community—lawyers, doctors, bankers, and successful businessmen. They walked, talked, and dressed like people who had money. Sometimes they even (especially their women) smelled like people who had money. They were the admired, or at least envied, bourgeois with respect to whom caddies were a money-hungry proletariat. Clearly, the members were living examples of what an ambitious young man might become if he didn't succumb to his instinctive playboy laziness. And there was the great satisfaction (actually a reversal of social roles) of being driven into town at the end of the day in a car the likes of which he could never hope to own and the owner of which was obliged not only to honor his request for a lift but to let him off at his preferred corner. Of course, as Marx might have told him, these perks were only the means the cunning system was using to seduce him into an uncritical cooperation.

In its own interest the system also inclined us to think of ourselves as valued contributors in our special world. Caddies treasured and often bragged about those moments when their employers treated them like fellow human beings, sought their advice about club selection or distance from the green, or praised their ability to find balls hit into deep rough. Most of the time, of course, one's golfer could be remote and uncommunicative enough, as if the caddy were simply a convenience attached to his golf bag. But there was always the possibility of caddying for one of those avuncular old-timers (usually a lousy golfer) who inquired about your off-course life, as if you were as entitled as he to have one. Even Lardner's tough-minded Dick prides himself on having a person-to-person relationship with the pretty Mrs. Doane. Lardner, of course, has little sympathy for such self-deception. His story assumes that Dick and his kind are no threat whatever to the system.

In fact, the system was designed to keep the caddy in his place at a respectful distance from his golfer. It was a rare and presumptuous caddy who dared to offer gratuitous advice to his golfer or praise him for a good shot. The decorum of the system kept the proletariat caddy from crossing into bourgeois territory, and at the same time relieved the caddy of the interpersonal responsibility that such a crossing over would entail. This anonymity was part of what made the caddy's life a lazy one. Your player might be having a miserable day, but unless you were inordinately tender-minded it was his burden, not yours. You got paid nevertheless, went home happy and slept well, having experienced none of the painful sympathy I had felt for my agent when I sensed that my performance as a Young Hustler did not measure up to his expectations for my future. At the same time, as any golfer knows, the game itself has a self-entrancing capacity to keep the caddy and a good deal else on the periphery of the golfer's attention. I have caddied for oblivious hackers who, I was sure, could not distinguish me from the other caddy in the foursome even after eighteen holes.

Anonymity, by releasing you from the burdensome obligations of intimacy, may be a great reinforcer of laziness, but among the nascent hoodlums in the caddy force—actually, an adolescent lumpen proletariat—it could also reinforce the need to be compensated for having been made anonymous. They took their revenge by pilfering golf balls and sometimes cigarettes and cigars from golf bags they were entrusted with. In the rough they might nudge a ball into an impossible lie and later regale their intimates with the ludicrous consequences. They made snide remarks about their golfers' personal habits and mimicked their eccentric swings. Even on the rare occasions when the hoodlums were tipped, the size of the tip was only proof that the tipper was a tightwad. They could be just as hard on their less disaffected fellow caddies, probably suspecting that they were secretly on the side of the bourgeois golfers. They would not scruple to eat a sack lunch that some guileless youngster had left on a bench in the caddy shack. They were, in short, blood brothers to those lumpen anarchists who had violated the decorum of our Young Hustler banquets.

If you know anything about golf you know that it is governed by a mystique of the rules. The rules are in their way tyrannous and must be so, given the possibilities for cheating that inhere in the physical distance between competing players. Nothing is more inspiring in the golfing world than a professional golfer's penalizing of himself (and perhaps giving up thousands of dollars in prize money) for an infraction of the rules that no one else could have seen. In Scott Fitzgerald's *The Great Gatsby* nothing underlines Jordan Baker's fundamental dishonesty more than the strong possibility that she cheated in a golf tournament. Lardner's Dick can be very priggish about the wealthy members who lie about their scores, even tipping the caddies who support their lies—though he admits that he fudged the rules in order to help the pretty Mrs. Doane get her ball out of the rough.

Most caddies quickly picked up this mystique of the rules and it became a fierce ethic with which they measured both their employers and their fellow caddies. A person who would lie about his score or improve his lie in the rough would do anything. This, of course, was the way it was with the hoodlums. You were a fool if you played them for a nickel a hole on the occasions when caddies were permitted on the course to play off the holes they earned weeding greens. It was as if the hoodlums had discovered early in life that the rules were designed to keep them subordinated to the bourgeois world in which Young Hustlers got all the breaks, and that unless a way around the rules could be found there was no life whatever for hoodlums. The spiritually lazy life of the caddy was ideal for them. In their primitive way, and often at considerable risk, they were extending the frontiers of experience, and so they were often secretly admired by ex-Young Hustlers who had lost faith in the rules but lacked the courage to violate them. In this perspective the hoodlums may help to explain why anti-bourgeois hoodlum jailbirds like the Frenchmen Jean Genet and the Marquis de Sade could become cult figures in literary circles.

Certainly the young hoodlums I caddied with often appeared to take great risks, but in time I came to suspect that they were the risks of least resistance, motivated not so much by an urge to extend the frontiers of experience as by a need to find an easy escape from the boring pressures of experience. Basically, they were utopians of laziness who had been beguiled into expecting that some benevolent force would keep the burden of the most likely future off their backs. Confident that there would always be someone else's lunch to eat, they were spared the burden of having to rise in the world. Later too I came to suspect that many hoodlums, and not all of them young, yearned subconsciously to be in jail, free at last from their crippling addiction to rule-breaking—and perhaps free, like Norman Mailer's onetime protégé Jack Abbott, to develop unsuspected talents in circumstances where they were subsidized by the rule-keeping bourgeois. At the same time, I came to see that a good deal of my own dissatisfaction with the life of a Young Hustler stemmed from the fact that in my heart I had not yet given up on the utopia of laziness.

In the meantime, in high school now and working summers in the wheat and cattle country of southeastern Washington, I had become addicted to the supplementary income of spring and fall caddying. I had acquired a collection of unmatched secondhand clubs and had managed to get my game into the eighties. There were times when I could imagine no better life than one centered on golf, though I never aspired, like Lardner's Dick, to become a pro. I had learned how to live comfortably with the hoodlums and at times even enjoy their company. Those among them who hadn't already been expelled from grade school were beginning to drop out of high school, having discovered, as they might have said a few generations later, that it was doing nothing for their self-esteem. Nevertheless, thanks to their free-wheeling cynicism about the hostile, uptight world, they could be entertaining in ways that straightlaced Young Hustler types could never be. If there were times when it seemed to me that the lazy life might go on forever, no doubt they were partly responsible.

But one fateful Saturday morning word came down from the caddymaster that our wages were being cut: we were to get ninety cents instead of a dollar-twenty for carrying two bags, seventy-five instead of ninety cents for carrying one. The caddies, who had planned their lives with absolute trust in the old pay scale, sat around in a state of shock. The hoodlums and their sympathizers were convinced that the true nature of those bourgeois tightwads, the club members, was finally out in the open for all to see. If we took this sitting down (which most of us were doing at the time) we would end up paying the members for the privilege of carrying their bags. Others were convinced that the toadying caddymaster had himself set the new rates in the expectation of increasing his own salary.

Soon the word spread around that we were going on strike, though who had decided this was not clear. Before long, however, we were all walking down the road, as if animated by a Hegelean world spirit, and settled on a hillside that overlooked the thirteenth fairway. No one seemed to know how all this had happened or what was supposed to happen next. It was as much a mystery to me as, years before, the dead man's muddied boots had been. Then the caddymaster arrived in a limousine with one of the club members. The latter, having learned what our grievance was, explained very civilly that the country had come on hard times, in fact there was a depression going on, and everyone was feeling the pinch, members no less than caddies. In response to someone's question how long this state of affairs would continue he was only able to say that he hoped not for long. In the meantime, he was sure that once we had thought the matter over we would return to our place of work—without prejudice, of course. Having said this, he and the caddymaster climbed into the limousine and left.

There was some mutinous grumbling as we sat there among the burgeoning spring flowers. Apparently the strike leaders, whoever they were, had no contingency plan. Perhaps, like lumpen proletariat everywhere, they had been unable to imagine any other response to their demands than instant and unconditional capitulation. There being no other way out of that boring impasse, a few bold ones started back to the clubhouse, and soon the rest of us were straggling unHegeleanly after them. A few malcontents (perhaps they were the real leaders) announced that they were washing their hands of the place and caught early rides to town. In a couple of weeks, however, they were back, probably having discovered that it was indeed hard times.

Life went on but the old lazy atmosphere did not survive the depression. Tips were fewer and smaller and a few members began to carry their own bags, perhaps to save money and at the same time advertise their bourgeois independence of the proletariat caddy force. The fact that a few of the new caddies who appeared on the scene were in their late twenties was an equally ominous sign. There was no more talk of a strike; instead there was a pervasive anxiety that our wages might be further reduced. It was, in short, a time when even the souls of ambitious Young Hustler types were sorely tried.

It was a bad time too for the malcontent young hoodlums. Being in love with laziness, they took the depression very seriously, since it smelled of a future in which laziness had come to an end. In fact, a few of them were separated from the caddy force for what amounted to conspicuous failures to behave like Young Hustlers. Perhaps some of them ended up in the ranks of the malcontent and Marxist-addicted left, having in those grim thirties been beguiled by its golden promises. Being both lumpen and lazy, they would have resonated to the image of the good life as they might have found it in Marx's *The German Ideology*: being able "to do one thing today and another tomorrow, to hunt in the morning, fish in the afternoon, rear cattle in the evening, criticize after dinner just as I have a mind." They would soon enough have discovered, however, that Marxists preferred recycled Young Hustler types who, being neither lumpen nor lazy, and certainly not critical, were good for the long haul and willing to put off the hunting and fishing for a while so that all could rise in the world together.

In the meantime the depression went on, summer ranch wages had decreased to a dollar a day, and the income from caddying, once a luxury, had become a grim necessity. In college now, I felt overqualified for such menial work. Trudging around the course with my two golf bags revived the sense of being trapped in a dead end that had burdened my terminal months as a Young Hustler. Fortunately, Franklin D. Roosevelt came to my rescue. Thanks to his National Youth Administration, my university was able to pay me for working as a library assistant. For a couple of hours every afternoon I checked in and checked out books. When business was slack, which it often was, I sat behind my desk and read Dickens, to whom I had become as addicted as in another life I had been to golf. For a while, with the burden of a dead-end future removed, I could enjoy in good conscience the best kind of lazy life.

Evil by a Damsite
1936 - 1938

s college graduation neared in the middle of the Great Depression, I was anticipating my annual return to the wheat and cattle country of southeastern Washington where I was assured of being paid for the kind of ranch work I was thoroughly familiar with and loved. Suddenly, however, I was offered a position with the MWAK, the acronym for the consortium of construction companies that was building Grand Coulee Dam in the middle of the state. Sensing that my life had come to a time of turning, I accepted the offer, and two days after graduation was at work as a checker in the grocery section of MWAK's department store. The salary was twenty-two dollars and fifty cents a week, not bad when one considered that down on the job many responsible and much more hazardous positions were paying only twice as much. Certainly, I would have milked cows, weeded summer fallow, and gone cowboying into the Snake River canyons for much less.

I was of course overeducated for my position, but this was too common a condition in those stringent times to impress me or anyone else. In fact, the very magnitude of the whole operation tended to distract one's attention from such meanly personal matters. Here about seven thousand men worked three shifts a day with an immense amount of spectacular machinery, all aimed at harnessing the mighty Columbia River so that it would supply electricity and irrigation to light up the land, empower the industry, and make the desert bloom—that wilderness in which, as William Cullen Bryant says in his poem "Thanatopsis," the Columbia, given its Indian name Oregon, "hears no sound/Save its own dashing." The Dam would require over ten million yards of concrete; when completed it would produce a falls twice as high as Niagara and back up a hundred-fifty-mile lake. The final phase, the High Dam, would cost over forty million depression dollars, probably enough now to finance another war in the Persian Gulf. When in September of 1935 President Roosevelt dedicated the Hoover Dam he called it "a twentieth century marvel," but we all knew that the Grand Coulee Dam would be the eighth wonder of the world and dwarf Cheops' pyramid. To be part of an enterprise of such magnitude, even as a grocery checker, was an exhilarating experience in ego-deflation.

In the process of hosing and servicing all these people a half-dozen towns had sprung up. Apart from the company town, Mason City, and Government Town across the river, these communities appeared to have been modeled on the mining and cattle towns in pre-World War II black-and-white movies. There were few such urban amenities as paved streets, sidewalks, and streetlights. Hard-working and hard-playing people, migrants of the construction world, lived and played in theses places. In the bars, where the liquor was cheap and plentiful, there was juke box music so that for ten cents you could rent the services of one of the taxi dancers, fresh-faced youngsters perhaps just out of high school, some of whom, I was told, could be persuaded to go upstairs with you for a bit more than ten cents. B Street in the town of Grand Coulee was notorious for its houses of prostitution. At my graduation the commencement speaker had warned us that we were going out into the real world and had to expect evils we were unfamiliar with but with which we should be able to cope thanks to values that had been instilled in us. I sometimes wondered if he could have spoken with such confidence if he had seen B Street on any Saturday night.

But there were evils closer to home for me. The company's cantonment in Mason City fed 1200 men a day in a great mess hall and housed them two to a bunkhouse. My own bunkhouse mate was an amiable veteran of Hoover Dam days who liked to write his wife after supper and then go out prowling with his buddies. Often he came in drunk, waking me with his racket, and perhaps vomiting on his clothes after he had deposited them on the floor between our beds. This being an evil I could not cope with, I moved into more expensive quarters outside the company compound. Here I fell among some Texans who had taken over an unused room for late-night poker parties to which I was genially invited. Unfortu-nately, penny-ante college poker had ill prepared me for the Texas sharpies. The second night I played they took me for two weeks' salary, so there was no more of that—though the Texans, who were no fools, kept inviting me.

Instead I began to spend my leisure time more virtuously in the recreation hall where there was one billiard table. In college I had become fascinated with three-cushion billiards and had obtained from the Brunswick Company a pamphlet explaining and diagramming the diamond system, a combination of arithmetic and geometry that unlocks the secrets of that grand game. There were a half-dozen other three-cushion fanatics in town, none of whom seemed to know that the twenty diamonds located along the four rails were more than decoration. I began to do to my opponents what the Texans had done to me, except that less money was involved: the losers simply had to pay the rent for the table. Soon I was the acknowledged champion of the Grand Coulee area. My disgusted victims often referred to me as Willie Hoppe, who, because he knew the diamond system, once ran twenty billiards in tournament play. The best I was ever able to manage was a run of three bank shots, one of them a five-cushion shot, which not only impressed.a handful of spectators but more than compensated for my embarrassment at poker.

My new roommate, who had early on warned me to have nothing to do with the Texans, had immediately struck me as a reliable, straight-shooting and plain-talking fellow who had come up the hard way and had no sympathy for the slackers, bullshitters, and complainers whom he saw as making up the bulk of mankind. He occasionally came in late at night, but always quietly and always sober. I doubted that his salary was much higher than mine but he owned an expensive and well-groomed coupe in which he sometimes drove me to Sunday mass. An absolutely secular man himself (in reaction, I gathered from a strict Protestant childhood), he nevertheless liked the idea that I was a regular churchgoer. Perhaps it suggested to him that I was a reliable character in a society peopled with time-servers and frauds. I had assumed that he was unmarried, but one Sunday after I returned from mass he said that he would like me to meet his wife. We drove up into the wilderness of B Street in Grand Coulee and went up through the unexpected Sunday quiet to the second floor of what I knew to be one of the more popular whorehouses.

His wife proved to be a slender, attractive woman who carried herself with grace and confidence. She took me into a sort of parlor and gave me scotch and soda while her husband went elsewhere, perhaps to look over the books. Knowing that I was a college man, and having herself spent some time at a state university, she wanted to talk about those finer things that college people had in common. She had loved to read, had in fact read Thomas Mann's *The Magic Mountain* (still in the future for me), but had especially been interested in the dance, by which she obviously did not mean taxi-dancing. I would have preferred to learn something about her attitude toward her present occupation: was she perhaps what in later years I would have identified as the Polly Adler or Mayflower Madam of B Street? But she said nothing about her work, whether out of respect for my innocence or because she assumed that for the moment at least she and I existed in an enclave abstracted away from such gross matters.

On the way back my friend was likewise silent about his extralegal second occupation, as if being men of the world we both understood that it was nothing more than a way to augment income in hard times. Perhaps if I had asked how he had gotten mixed up in such an evil business he would have said what F. Scott Fitzgerald's Jay Gatsby says when Nick Carraway asks him how that crook Myer Wolfsheim managed to fix the World Series: "He just saw the opportunity." He might have assumed too that Catholics were much more relaxed about such defections from conventional morality. In any event, I learned some years later that he ended up in the penitentiary, having been caught transporting girls across state lines (a practical necessity in his business). There was no word about his wife. I hoped that she had seen the reversal as an opportunity to return to the university and pick up where she had left off with her reading and the dance.

Soon in the interest of saving money I went downstream a few miles to another ramshackle bedroom community and moved in with a group of fellow workers from the company store. When this ménage became uncomfortably crowded I moved again, this time into a nearby one-room cabin, which I rented from a local barber for ten dollars a month. Living like Thoreau now, I cooked my own meals and had the solitude I needed to write the weekly column I was contributing to the diocesan Catholic newspaper. At night when there was nothing else to do I lay on my bunk reading my only book, the complete plays of William Shakespeare. Now in the late summer afternoons there was time to run down to my private Walden Pond, the Columbia River, and practice my Australian crawl. I swam out to and around a little island located about forty yards offshore. The real test of strength then was to swim across the river, and occasionally tanned and frolicsome young men did so, going in groups of three or four. I was teased with the possibility of doing it myself after I had gotten in shape but gave up the idea when I learned that two swimmers in a party of four had been caught in the treacherous midstream currents and drowned. Many years later I visited the area with my children, wanting to show them my island. Not only did it no longer exist but the wonderful wildness of the shoreline was gone, as if when the engineers had finished with their Dam they couldn't resist a final opportunity to demonstrate their mastery of the mighty river.

If there was any opportunity in my position with the MWAK I did not see it. Like so many things one did during the Great Depression, it pointed to nothing beyond itself. It paid a living wage so that I could afford to write my weekly column, which paid me nothing. The checker's job was neither challenging nor creative. One had to be able to handle money quickly (I had already learned to do that as a racetrack parimutuel cashier), keep the cash register in balance, and remember prices (no problem for one who in high school had been required daily to memorize twenty lines of Virgil's *Aeneid*). However, there was the compensation of human interest. A grocery checker in that rough-and-tumble community was in the position of bartender: he got to know everybody, picked up the current gossip, scandalous and jejune, and on occasion was expected to function as confidant and father confessor, especially in the middle of the day when business was slow.

One morning, for instance, a swing-shift jackhammer operator lingered tentatively at the checkout counter after paying for his groceries. Normally he shopped with his wife, a handsome woman, and their small son, and I'd always enjoyed chatting with them. Now I sensed uneasily that he was about to tell me something I'd just as soon not hear. He'd recently made a date with someone else's wife, he said, but at the moment of truth discovered that he was for the first time in his life impotent. I had of course read about such things in books—even in those remote times you could find anything in a book. Besides, I had heard all about the mores of the community: with three shifts a day there was ample opportunity for this sort of extracurricular entertainment, night shift men being especially likely to be cuckolded. But I had never been face to face with a man who confessed to adultery, or at least an attempt at it, particularly when he had such an attractive wife whom he apparently loved. The contradiction put me back in the whorehouse with the Madam who had a taste for finer things. I did not know what face to put on the matter: was I in the presence of tragedy, comedy, or farce? Had he failed, the man wondered ruefully, because he had felt so damned guilty? Out of the depths of my college man's ignorance I agreed that guilt was the likely explanation. A few days later when the three of them came through the checkstand they seemed normally happy together, and I could only assume that the guilt and the impotence were gone.

I also had to serve as confidant to the other checker, an ingratiating young man who spent a good deal of time caressing the wave in his blond hair, and who when business was slow gave me detailed reports of his sexual exploits, perhaps to let me know that there could be life abundant even for a man who hadn't been to college. He was much taken by a vivacious young wife who appeared daily with her pre-school youngster. He considered her the most beautiful woman he had ever seen and was unhappy when she came through my side of the checkstand. Then for several days she did not appear. One morning he gave me the appalling news that she had died suddenly after an abortion, the consequence of an affair that she had been carrying on for some months. He kept shaking his head at the incomprehensible monstrosity of it: she had died being so beautiful. I thought of Edgar Allen Poe's definition of "the most poetical topic in the world," the death of a beautiful woman, but had the tact not to refer to it, sensing that what he was experiencing was not poetry but, perhaps for the first time in his life, the tragic complexity of good and evil.

So it was the real world truly enough, and anything but dull. Meanwhile my billiard game was improving and so was my Australian crawl. On Sundays I could go hiking up the tawny ravines above the river or go down river a few miles to the Nespelem Indian reservation where a primitive golf course had been carved out of the wilderness. I explored as much of the Dam itself as a man without a badge and a hardhat had access to. One Sunday I discovered an entrance to the eight miles of exquisitely tailored service galleries that honeycombed the mighty structure. I saw no one as I wandered around in that great netherworld, uneasily aware that I was out of bounds. The only sound was the muted roar of the overrushing river, how far above me now, hearing nothing but its own dashings, I could only guess. I was to remember the sensation of being down there years later as my wife and I roamed late in a May afternoon through Père-Lachaise cemetery in Paris looking for the grave of Oscar Wilde.

Distinguished visitors were always appearing on the scene. One morning the word was that James A. Farley, the Postmaster General, was standing in front of the local post office shaking hands with one and all. I went down there and stood in line to shake his rather limp hand. President Roosevelt arrived: we all went to see him tour up the main street and then crowded into the public square to listen to his enthusiastic approval of what we were doing. Later on such notables as Thomas Dewey, Harry Truman, Prince Olaf of Norway, General Jonathan Wainwright, and even Hailie Selassie of Ethiopia showed up. To us who were natives of the Damsite, in fact, distinguished visitors were an expected commonplace: who would not want to see the Eighth Wonder of the World?

To me, however, the most memorable visitor was, at least when he arrived, distinguished for nothing. This was a lean hawk-faced young man with intense eyes who showed up in the store one morning with a college classmate of mine and said that he wanted to talk to me about some urgent business as soon as possible. Since it was time for my midday break, I went with them to the company restaurant to confer over coffee. The stranger had come to town on fire with a plan: the publication of a weekly newspaper that would serve the Damsite not simply by publishing construction statistics and piddling local gossip in competition with the already established papers (about which he had the lowest possible opinion) but by telling the real truth about the place. There was no indication that he had been in the area long enough to know anything about it, but he had no doubt that it was ripe for and badly needed a first-class muckraking. Having learned from my friend that I had edited a college newspaper and was already an established writer, he saw me as the logical person to edit his paper. Given the intensity of his eyes and the sense he gave of being on fire with a mission the integrity of which was beyond question, I could only say that I was interested. Which in a way I was: writing for publication was always interesting, especially if, as at this point I assumed, there was money involved.

I met with him three or four times, always during my midday break and always over coffee in the restaurant. His invariable companion was a tall redhead who contributed little to the conversation but seemed utterly enthralled with our charismatic leader. What part he was to play in our enterprise was never clear, but perhaps it was enough that he owned an old Plymouth touring car. Where our leader was living was not clear, but he and the redhead apparently spent most of their time scouting around the Damsite looking for examples of the evil that was to be our business.

Of this he had found God's plenty, certainly more than enough to validate the warnings of the most pessimistic commencement speaker: local merchants gouging the public; landlords renting their clapboard shacks for exorbitant figures; the contractors wasting government money and doing a slipshod job to boot; apparently respectable functionaries shacking up with workers' wives; apparently respectable wives using their swing-shift freedom to take on all comers; the lives of construction workers being callously sacrificed to keep on schedule a project that was an appalling boondoggle; innocent young women being virtually enslaved in the cathouses of B Street. He was especially incensed by the corruptions of the latter place; exposing it would have to be one our first concerns, an uneasy prospect for me given a residual loyalty to my old roommate and his refined wife.

Of course none of this would have been startling news to anyone who had been in the area a few months. What elevated it above the level of checkstand gossip and gave it urgency was the mad intensity of the speaker's eyes and the barely contained fury of his voice as he recounted some new moral atrocity. He was a true cacophiliac, a man in love with an ideal vision of badness. Like so many people I got to know in later years, especially in the sixties and seventies, he had apparently learned that the quickest way to feel virtuously alive was to discover evil, and having made that discovery he was hooked on evil, was in fact a cacoholic. If he had run out of badness he would, like the Marquis de Sade or Milton's Satan, have run out of life.

But his cacoholia had its effect on me by creating an atmosphere in which I was not inclined to ask nitpicking questions: When was all this going to begin? Who was going to do all the writing? Where would the start-up money come from? Was I to have a salary so that I could give up my job as a checker? Nothing our charismatic leader ever said offered a clue to the answer of any of these questions. Perhaps it was the impression he gave of an immense but unspecified familiarity not only with the newspaper world but the world in general that ruled out as naively premature any consideration that would muddy up the abstract grandeur of our enterprise. The only concession he made to mundane realities was a remark that the local merchants would of course fall all over themselves to advertise in our paper—the same merchants, presumably, whom we would expose as price gougers and retailers of shoddy merchandise.

In our third meeting the redhead drove us to one of the neighboring communities where our leader expected to meet the mayor and get the lowdown on some civic corruption, exactly what he did not say. He went around to the back of the mayor's not especially mayoral shanty while I waited with the redhead in the car. After a while our leader returned, his eyes flashing with pent-up rage: it was the mayor's afternoon to be with his girlfriend. They drove me back to work and I agreed to meet with them in three days. Now that we knew what we were doing, our leader said, we could at least get down to particulars.

Under the circumstances no particulars were imaginable. Three days went by,

then a week, without word from either of them. One morning I received my first-
ever telegram, a long day letter from somewhere in Idaho. Here were particulars at
last. I was directed to ignore all previous plans for the first issue, move the story
about construction deaths to the first page, put the story about B Street prostitution
on page two, confine all local gossip to the middle of the paper, and put all ads on
the back page. But particular as all this sounded there was still the question of how
one was to locate or relocate nonexistent stories in a hypothetical newspaper for
which no ads had been sold. There was nothing to do but wait for more particulars.
None ever came; I never saw either of them again. About a month later my old
college friend came visiting again and apologized for the trouble he had caused me.
My world-reforming leader with the mad eyes had cast his spell over my friend, too,
but subsequent information had put those eyes in a different perspective for him.
The man had escaped from an asylum in southern Idaho and was now back in
custody, having turned himself in or been captured. I preferred to believe that he
had gone back voluntarily to the familiar evils of the madhouse, having learned that
he could not cope with the exotic evils of the real world he had created. And I began
to understand, too, why it had never occurred to me to ask where he had come from
or what in particular he had done for a living: as if I had sensed that he was a kind
of avenging spirit whose proper home and place of business was wherever evil was,
which was everywhere.

In any event, it was a relief to be rid of the burden of having to reform the
wicked world. I could give my undivided attention to three-cushion billiards and my
Australian crawl, and spend more time with Shakespeare, where there were evils
enough to satisfy the most rabid cacoholic. Fall and winter passed uneventfully and
early in spring my salary went up to twenty-five dollars a week. But the more I
though of the coming summer the more I began to sense that I was coming again to
a time of turning. So I gave up my checker's job and returned one more time to the
wheat and cattle country, climbed on my favorite horse, and rode again into my
kind of wilderness: the wonderful Snake River canyons. I like to think that my lost
leader, a few hundred miles to the south and in a haven now where his cacophilia
could be lovingly tended to, was just as happily at work revising his imaginary
newspaper as I was when I rode into rock-tumbled ravines looking for strayed cattle.

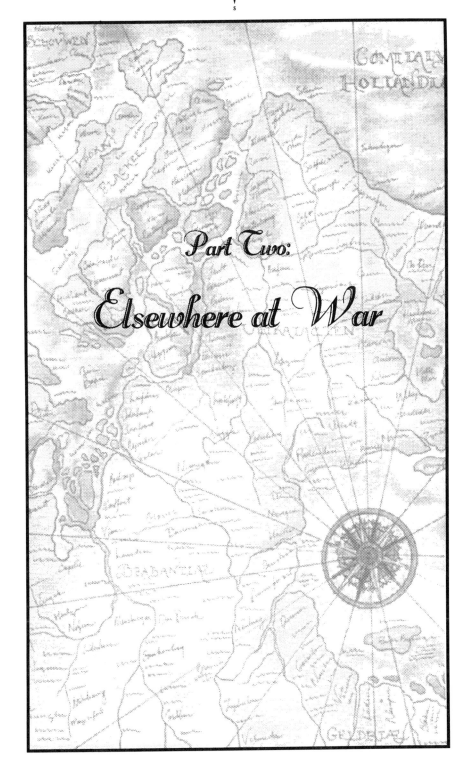

Part Two:

Elsewhere at War

At War with General Forrest
1942 - 1946

Here, too, the honorable finds its due
and there are tears for passing things;
here, too, things mortal touch the mind.

y life with the late General Nathan Bedford Forrest was in
its beginnings a matter of illiteracy in Tennessee. Not
that the General, a Tennessee man, was in any way
illiterate. On the contrary, he had been well schooled at
Georgia Tech and West Point. Nor do I mean to imply
that I agree with those who were or still are convinced that
his famous great-grandfather, that other General Nathan Bedford
Forrest, was illiterate. It is true, of course, that the latter had no formal
schooling. President Zachary Taylor's son Richard, who met him toward the end of
the Civil War, said that Forrest read with difficulty. His biographer, John Allen
Wyeth, tells us that he always said "betwixt" and "fetch," and "mout" and "fit"
when he meant "might" and "fought." Like Keats and F. Scott Fitzgerald, he had
trouble with his spelling. To judge from his military correspondence, however, he
was as literate as his peers, Robert E. Lee, Stonewall Jackson, and William
Tecumseh Sherman, all of whom had the advantage of West Point and were even, at
one time or another, academic people. Nevertheless, since it is as useful to his
admirers as to his detractors, the legend of his total or near illiteracy dies hard, so
that if he did not really say that his military principle was "to get there fustest with
the mostest" (Henry Steele Commager, among others, believes that he really said "to
get there first with the most men") he should have said it. But whatever he said, the
illiteracy that led me to the Forrests was a pure accident of war.

The "fustest" General Forrest and I both enlisted as privates, he in Captain Josiah White's Tennessee Mounted Rifle Company, I in the 117th Guard Squadron at Fort George Wright in Spokane, Washington, which at the time was headquarters for the Second Air Force. What Private Forrest brought with him to the rifle company is not recorded. All I brought with me, apart from bare living necessities, was the two-volume Random House Proust. I was determined that if I survived the war (which in the fall of 1942 seemed unlikely) I would not come home culturally empty-handed. My fellow guards, mainly Kentucky hill people and Mexican-Americans, were exactly the sort of soldiers who would have driven the great Civil War general mad: undedicated, unreliable, bungling, but amiable. They went to sleep on post, got lost in the dark, shot themselves accidentally, forgot their general orders and passwords, and lived in apprehension of the black panther which some of them swore they had seen at night in the woods around the north gate. If there was a wrong way to do something, said our often-disgusted training sergeant, the guards would, by God, be the first to try it out. At one time, in fact, seven of the thirteen inmates of the guardhouse were members of the Guard Squadron, so that there was an inbred quality about the whole security enterprise.

In time, I was promoted to private first class and assigned to base headquarters as assistant squadron payroll clerk. The job was easy enough, but it lacked challenge and promise of promotion. Thus the base training officer, having learned that I had been a college teacher, easily persuaded me to take over an evening class of fifteen or so illiterate Tennessee boys. Not being very literate about the problems of illiteracy, I began the course with a series of lectures on the history of the English language. After the first lecture, a story about the great thing I was doing appeared in the local paper; after the second, I was summoned to the office of the adjutant general of the Second Air Force. He had seen the news story, in which I was identified as an expert in written and spoken communication, and wondered if I was not exactly the person they were looking for. The command had been criticized for the poor quality of its official prose, and it was decided that someone would have to be put in charge of outgoing communication. Would I like to be that person? The alternative of the illiteracy class was suddenly intolerable. I accepted the offer, and the adjutant general suggested that I report immediately to General Forrest, the chief of staff.

I went down the long corridor to the chief of staff's office and hardly had time to catch my breath there before the blond, motherly secretary ushered me into the General's office. He was the first general I had ever seen in the flesh. Fortunately, I did not yet know of his relationship to that other General Forrest, so that I was only moderately nervous as I stood in front of his desk. He was a handsome man with skeptical, brooding eyes and a trim brush mustache. He had come to Spokane the previous year with the Fifth Bombardment Group, was transferred to the Second Air Force as operations officer, and soon was chief of staff, at thirty-six one of the youngest general officers in the country. In little more that a year, he had gone from major to brigadier—not quite keeping pace with his great-grandfather, who, despite the handicap of his forty years, progressed between June 1861 and June 1862 from private to brigadier.

I did not salute the General as I stood there. So far, I had not saluted lieutenants, captains, the only major I had gotten close to, and, on my seconds day with Guard Squadron, the disgusted first sergeant. But nothing n my ramshackle basic training had prepared me for a general. He gave me his frosty little smile and repeated in his terse and clipped style what the adjutant general had already told me. In effect, I was to be assistant chief of staff for military composition. In order to put myself in the picture, I was to have access to the safe in the outer office so that I could read the records of the Second Air Force. It was then late in the morning. He suggested that I take the rest of the day off in order to move out of the Guard Squadron. Still not saluting, I left him.

So I went back to base and cleared out of the bungling Guard Squadron. The first sergeant shook hands with me and predicted a great future. The chief payroll clerk was convinced that I would be immediately promoted to staff sergeant; anything else, he said, would be an affront to the General. I collected my gear and moved into one of the headquarters barracks, where the literacy rate was obviously much higher and where a man might lie on his bunk reading Proust without feeling that he was making a spectacle of himself. In fact, in the next barracks, there was an aspiring writer who was doomed in time to hang himself, though not before he had persuaded me to read a good deal of the chaotic novel he was working on. Within a week I was promoted to corporal, the highest noncommissioned rank I was ever to achieve. Meanwhile, the class of Tennessee illiterates was left stranded half way through the history of the English language. Eventually, I learned, a buck sergeant who had taught English in high school took it over.

Now it was winter, early 1943. Roosevelt flew to Casablanca to confer with Churchill; British bombers struck Berlin for the first time in daylight; the Japanese were beaten in Guadalcanal, as were the Germans in Stalingrad. In the warmth and quiet of the General's outer office, I worked my way through the confidential, secret, and top-secret files of the Second Air Force. It was a young but burgeoning enterprise, possessing only 389 aircraft of all descriptions when I joined it, but already in the process of spreading over most of the West and Midwest. Its mission was to train the heavy bomber crews that manned the B-17's and B-24's in the European and African theaters; later it would train B-29 crews for the Pacific. Though I could not know it at the time, I was reading the prologue to Kiel, Dresden, Cassino, Ploesti, and Hiroshima. Much of the literature was incomprehensible to a layman, but I read it all scrupulously, and within two weeks I had acquired some kind of feel for the whole complex business. In the evenings, meanwhile, I was beginning to get the feel of Proust's even more complex business. Once or twice I went slumming back to the Guard Squadron. One of the Kentucky boys who had been stationed in a hospital ward to guard a sick prisoner had gone to sleep sitting upright in a chair and was now in the guardhouse; the Mexicans were still having trouble with general orders; the black panther was more that ever on their minds now that his spoor could be seen in the snow. Nothing had changed; they were losers; I was well rid of them.

II

On my first official day with him, the General told me in his curt but by no means unfriendly manner what his long-range plans for me were. After a novitiateship in his outer office, he would send me to Officers Candidate School at Miami Beach so that I could return as an officer to be his aide. This was astonishing news. Surely generals did not choose their aides so haphazardly. Why wouldn't he wait a prudent interval until he had had a chance to see whether I could measure up? I wondered if the eyes of headquarters operatives had been on me all along, if they had been checking me out with their hugger-mugger devices while I went my innocent way with the bungling guards? In any event, my future, which had previously been all uncertainty, now took definite if uneasy shape as my old apprehension that I was not meant to survive the war was reinforced by a new one: I had no idea what was required of an aide.

It was not long after this announcement that I learned from the blond secretary the true identity of the General. Indeed, without realizing it, I had already seen the clear signs of that identity in the folder of his desk: the two generals facing each other, just as they would a few months later in *Time*, strikingly resembling each other as everyone inevitably said, the great-grandfather suggesting the more formidable and commanding presence (the very ideal of a *beau sabreur* as Wyeth says), but the great-grandson looking formidable in his own way, no doubt in part because of the juxtaposition of the photograph. It was unthinkable not to salute such a man, but I had not saluted him yet (would I have to begin saluting him when I became his aide?). In fact, the only Tennesseean that I ever felt strongly compelled to salute was my first sergeant when, some years later and through another accident of war, I became troop commander at the Air Transport Command installation in British Guiana. He was only twenty-two, but he had that capacity to command instant obedience that both Forrests would have appreciated.

Knowing the General's relationship to that "devil, Forrest" put the failure to salute him into a nervous historic context. Worse, I soon learned that since becoming chief of staff he had acquired the reputation of being something of a devil in his own right. In those days the occupational disease of the Air Force was a prideful nonchalance about regulations, which was no doubt connected with its efforts to define itself against the older components of the armed forces. In headquarters this attitude displayed itself in a casual slovenliness, the signs of which were unshined shoes, tarnished brass, failure to salute or come to attention, exotic and unauthorized combinations of attire, much loitering around water coolers, and a great deal of aimless if good-natured drifting about from office to office. Such a state of affairs was apparently what Forrest had set out to correct. Now, in any event, there was much saluting and an at least superficial concentration on official business; officers dressed less eccentrically and enlisted men shined their shoes more often; attention was called whenever the General entered headquarters and everyone in the corridor snapped to attention.

All of this was still a far cry from the military termagancy of his great-grandfather—who, Wyeth reports, showed no mercy to cowards and ordered his officers to shoot anyone who flickered. Once he leaped from his horse to seize a trooper who was running away from battle, thrashed him with a stick, and forced him back into line. Nevertheless, there was the usual muttering among the headquarters noncoms about this new relatively tense and spruced-up state of affairs: the General's promotion had gone to his head, he had gotten himself confused with his glamorous ancestor, he was trying to turn the place into a Marine barracks, etc. On the other hand, there was general agreement among officers and noncoms that Forrest was a man of extraordinary competence who was being groomed for great things.

Both generals had commanding aristocratic appearances, but the great-grandson
had the advantage of being socially beyond question: not only was he West Point,
but he trailed history grandly behind him. His great-grandfather, however, had no
history to trail: he was known to be the son of a blacksmith and was himself a dirt
farmer, a man with no formal education and no social status to speak of. What one
of his aristocratic troopers wrote in his diary was no doubt the opinion of many:

. . .and I must express my distaste to being commanded by a man having no
pretension of gentility—a Negro trader, gambler,—and ambitious man, careless of the
lives of his men so long as preferment be in prospectus. Forrest may be & no doubt
is, the best Cav officer in the West, but I object to [that] tyrannical, hotheaded
vulgarian's commanding me.

Had Wyeth read this remark, he would have said that it was hardly typical.
Forrest out in front of his troops, urging them on with a bull voice that not even the
cannon could drown out; swinging his great sword, eyeballs, cheeks, and neck
swollen with the blood of rage; utterly careless of his own safety as he struck terror
into his foes and inspired his command to superhuman achievement—how was
there room for anything but admiration and awe for such a man? In hand-to-hand
combat he killed thirty men; twenty-nine horses were shot out from under him,
three at Fort Pillow alone; he was wounded or injured a half dozen times; he was
one of the greatest strategists and tacticians of all times. No wonder General
Sherman, himself something of a *beau sabreur*, said that Forrest must be taken "if it
costs 10,000 lives and breaks the Treasury." I see him as a kind of super Vince
Lombardi for whom anything short of total victory was intolerable and whose nature
it was to inspire strong ambivalent feelings in his subordinates. If such a man had
come into Second Air Force Headquarters, we would not only have snapped to
attention; we would have remained petrified in his electric wake long after he had
passed by.

The military composition was no great problem. I warmed up by rewriting a
few ambiguous general orders, then spent several days rewriting a brief but horribly
written manual that had been prepared by the training people on the second floor.
Then I was given a letter addressed to a senator refusing his request that a certain
co-pilot, ready to depart for England with the rest of his crew, be released from
service so that he might take over the management of the family ranch from his

ailing father. Someone upstairs had prepared this letter for the General's signature, but he wanted no part of it, sensing that even a stupid senator was likely to take it as an insult. He conferred briefly with me: the answer had to be a categorical but by all means delicate "No," since then as now the last thing the Air Force wanted to do was antagonize a legislator. I prepared the letter in an hour and a half, emphasizing the disrupting effects of replacements at the crucial state of departure for overseas, and it then became the model for similar refusals, though how it got disseminated among other offices I never knew.

In between editing and rewriting I went back to browsing among the secret documents or did small chores for the little brunette who shared the outer office. Her sole job was to transcribe the Dictaphone recordings of all conversations that came over the tactical phone lines. Hour by hour she sat at her typewriter listening to her headphones as the chief of staff or the commanding general (then Davenport Johnson) carried on their transactions with Generals Arnold or Spaatz or with the widely separated wing commanders of the Second Air Force. A suppressed squeal from her was always a sign that the generals were sounding less like generals and more like common soldiers, and then her job (a version of mine) was to make them sound more like generals again. Sometimes, in the interest of picking up more background, I read over her transcripts, trying to imagine what crudities were buried under her girlish euphemisms. Certainly the transcripts represented the General as measuring up to the high standard set by his great-grandfather, who, says Wyeth, might use violent language in the heat of battle but otherwise abhorred obscene or vulgar words and under no circumstances would "permit a smutty story to be told or a vulgar expression used in his presence."

It took me almost a month to realize what I should have expected all along: socially I existed in no man's land, a figure of suspicion and even resentment among headquarters personnel, whether officers or enlisted men. One of my few friends, a sergeant in personnel who bunked near me, first alerted me to my predicament. He had heard from another sergeant how the major who had written the letter to the senator, and who also had had a hand in the training manual, had reacted to my rewrite of the letter. "Who the hell's doing this?" the major demanded, piqued to discover that what had been good enough all along was suddenly unacceptable. "They've got a damn corporal down there," the sergeant told him. So I began to feel like that damned corporal, though I would have preferred to feel like a damned sergeant. I came to believe that they were hating me instead of the

General, or along with him, just as Major J. P. Strange had no doubt been hated along with *his* General Forrest simply because he had been the latter's adjutant, and hating me to boot because I had been a college professor who was now in a position to shove their miserable prose down their throats, and they couldn't do a damned thing about it except mutter to their sergeants because they were afraid to mutter to me or Forrest. Thus in effect I was ostracized and was therefore able to spend more time on my bunk with that unhappy man, M. Swann and, until he hung himself from his upper bunk, with the aspiring novelist.

The important thing was that the General was satisfied. Soon I was even collaborating with him in the phrasing of his unofficial correspondence. He had an excellent sense of language and knew immediately when an expression was just right for his purpose, even though he had no particular ability to bring it to that point himself. It no more bothered his West Point pride to lean on the support of a damned corporal than it had bothered his great-grandfather when Major Strange corrected his spelling or changed "fit" to "fought."

It was strange to learn ultimately that my reserved and dedicated General had a playful side. Periodically, the blond secretary would contact a certain lieutenant and make arrangements with him to meet the General for squash. It occurred to me one day that when I became his aide I might be expected to play squash with him, a game about which I knew absolutely nothing. Whatever problems Major Strange had with *his* General Forrest, it was not this one. Such playtime as the latter had (always, said a neighbor, yelling louder than anyone else) was over in his sixteenth year when at his father's death he "took the burden of life" as head of a family that included his mother, seven brothers, and three sisters. The only games he played after that were those grim charades that so effectively bamboozled the likes of Colonel Abel Streight and General Sooy Smith.

III

Spring of 1943 was at hand. The Americans were recovering some lost ground in Tunisia; the Japanese finally abandoned the Guadalcanal area; the Royal Air Force hit Berlin hard; I finished *Swann's Way* and began *Within A Budding Grove* at about the same time that the Guard Squadron's black panther was demythologized into a brown mongrel dog and the would-be novelist hung himself with three knotted-together G. I. neckties. With startling suddenness then, orders came to proceed to Officers Candidate School. One of my few friends predicted that I would immediately be promoted to staff sergeant since I would need the extra income at OCS. I went in to see the General for the last time and for the last time did not salute him. Instead he shook my hand, and as he did so I realized not only that I had come to like him very much but that I was about to leave my pleasantly ostracized job for very doubtful gain. Nevertheless, I put Proust away and went off obediently to Miami Beach. En route I passed through Rome, Georgia, not far from where that devil Forrest, with the assistance of spunky Emma Sansom who led him to the lost cattleford on Black Creek, finally took the measure of Colonel Abel Streight's Raiders.

Miami Beach in those days had been pretty well taken over by the military for training and schooling operations. The few remaining civilians stood out like rare animals in a zoo. We lived in resort hotels, drilled and exercised on the golf course, and ate in night clubs from which signs of sybaritic and even pornographic luxury had not been entirely erased. Major and minor celebrities—movie stars, professional ball players, a few writers, social register aristocrats who had somehow missed direct commissions—were scattered indiscriminately among the OCS squadrons. Even Clark Gable, who was subsequently assigned to the Second Air Force for gunnery training, had been there. Squadron Eleven, my squadron, had the movie star John Carroll, now long forgotten but then at the peak of his career as a romantic singing Latin. He was the unofficial music master of the squadron, which was expected to sing constantly in all marching formations. He was a handsome and agreeable fellow who several times complimented me on my singing, something no one had ever done before or would ever do again. When he graduated a class ahead of me, he came around to give me his left-over textbooks.

No amount of singing could make us forget that OCS was at best hot, hellish, and anxious. Supposing that you made it to a commission (which seemed highly unlikely during the first six weeks) there remained the burning questions: Where would you be assigned? What would be your duties? OCS prepared you for everything and nothing. My advantage was therefore very great, knowing as I did where I would go and what I would do. I even gave out this information, in an offhand sort of way, to my three roommates, with the result that they looked at me with the respect they had previously reserved for John Carroll. They predicted that I would very quickly become a captain since the General's own prestige would be involved. I was tempted to believe this, though against it was the fact that I was still a damned corporal who had twice been led to believe that he would be much more.

But when the assignment sheet came out just before graduation, I was listed for Eastern Flying Training Command Headquarters at Maxwell Field in Montgomery, Alabama. I asked the officer who distributed the list if the assignment could be a mistake. The list was correct, he said, and the next evening, no longer a damned corporal but now an utterly abandoned second lieutenant, I climbed onto a daycoach and rode all night and most of the next day through the Dixie I was later to become so familiar with. No quarters were available at Maxwell Field; I was told to find accommodations in town. There the better hotels were filled with newly arrived and similarly disoriented officers. Eventually, I got a spacious but nondescript room in an old hotel far down Dexter Street. I stayed there three nights; after the second, I learned from an officer in personnel that the place was generally believed to be a whorehouse. Given my abandoned condition, it seemed appropriate enough.

But I did not give up hope. Perhaps Maxwell Field was only a staging area in a process that would eventually return me to the Second Air Force and General Forrest; at any moment the order might come; there was even hope in the fact that Maxwell Field did not seem to know what to do with me. No orders came; I was assigned to Spence Field in Moultrie, Georgia, as a special service officer, where in due time I picked up the auxiliary chores of WAC recruiting officer and army emergency relief officer. I sent for Proust and settled down to make the best of my bad lot.

I had not been at Spence Field a week before I learned that I had been orphaned, not abandoned. In the officer's club one evening, I was browsing through *Time* when, shockingly, there were my two Generals at the bottom of a page, separated by a column of print but otherwise looking exactly as they had looked on the chief of staff's desk. He had gone along as an observer in a raid over Kiel, saying in effect what his great-grandfather had said in his farewell address to his troops: "I have never on the field of battle sent you where I was not willing to go myself." The plane had been hit; eight of the ten-man crew were seen to bail out as it went down in flames; Forrest was not one of them. Later I learned that he had left Fort Wright under secret orders in late May or early June. The Kiel raid had been on June 13, so that when I graduated from OCS he had been missing for two weeks, childless, and the last of his line. What had happened was obvious enough: once he was away from headquarters and unlikely to return, my enemies had seen to it that the damned corporal did not return either. There were moments when I envied the hanged novelist.

I settled into the long hot summer of the deep Jim Crow South. Allied troops under Eisenhower invaded Sicily; Syracuse fell; the Nineteenth Air Force bombed Rome, putting into practice tactics that in another lifetime had been part of my background reading; Mussolini resigned. I learned that the Second Air Force, as if determined to dissociate itself from my very memories, had moved its headquarters to Colorado Springs. If I had been able to go with it, I would have been only a few miles from the home where my paternal grandfather had lived for many years, the final twenty blind, and where at the age of ninety-two he had died, one of the last Civil War veterans in the West. As a boy of eighteen, he had enlisted with Company K, 45th Illinois, First Brigade, Third Division. He saw action at Kenesaw Mountain and Antietam, was with Sherman at the burning of Atlanta and during his great march to the sea, and later marched in the Grand Review at Washington D.C. He had been raised in New England so that there was no question of *his* literacy. When I saw him for the first and last time two years before his death, he sang Union marching songs for us in an eerie quavering voice and remembered how, as they marched through Georgia, the girls had cheered and waved at them. What did they have to cheer about? I wondered, and suspected, that the old man was in his own small way rewriting history. It did not occur to me to ask him about General Forrest, for the latter had not yet entered my life. "After all," said Sherman, "I think Forrest was the most remarkable man our Civil War produced on either side." It is conceivable that my grandfather, as one of Sherman's men, shared his commanding general's conviction; but it is just as conceivable that he had known only of that bloody massacring devil whose cavalry, Sherman complained bitterly, could go one hundred miles while his own was trying to go ten.

Moultrie, Georgia, was not Forrest country, but the farther reaches of the Eastern Flying Training Command extended into the Western Theater of the Civil War, which was rich with his memory. He had never gotten to Montgomery itself, though he might have gone there in the spring of 1865 in pursuit of General James Wilson after the latter had whipped him at Selma. At Selma, fifty miles west of Montgomery, the attraction had been the Confederate arsenal, and it was in protection of it that (although as usual badly outnumbered) he had made such a fool of General Sooy Smith the previous spring in northeastern Mississippi. There his brother Jeffrey had been killed, and there Forrest had made another of his miraculous escapes, killing three of the enemy in the process and as usual losing his horse.

It would therefore have been nice to go to Selma, where there was an airbase, but I never got there. It would have been better still to go up to the site of Fort Pillow on the Mississippi above Memphis. Here Forrest brought off one of his most remarkable victories, indeed, one of the most remarkable accomplishments in the history of cavalry warfare. Forrest himself estimated that the storming of this stronghold cost him only twenty men to the enemy's 500, so that, as he reported to his superior, General Polk, "the river was dyed with blood of the slaughtered for 200 yards." Unfortunately, Fort Pillow was also his Mai Lai, for among the dead was a vast number of black troops, and Forrest was accused, falsely, he believed, of permitting or ordering a massacre. I might have gotten there if I had been able to hitch a ride to Memphis, where after the war Forrest had served as a member of the Board of Aldermen, and where he is buried in front of the equestrian statue. But no one was ever flying that way when I was free to go. Instead, I went off to Atlanta, now long recovered from Sherman's depredations, to buy recreational supplies. There I thought of my young grandfather. Had he been present at Sherman's congratulatory address to his troops after the capture of Atlanta? Heard him prophesy "that our country will in time emerge from this war, purified from the fires of war?" Seen Atlanta burning? Been one of Uncle Billy's foragers, or "bummers," as the mighty horde swept through Georgia to the sea?

IV

So in the South it was possible to fight two wars at once; in fact, it was all too easy in southern Georgia—lush with cotton, tobacco, pecans, watermelons, and peaches—to forget all about the war immediately at hand. Nevertheless, it went on. Roosevelt, Churchill, and Stalin met at Teheran; Eisenhower (a far cry from Forrest) became supreme commander in Europe; the Red Army entered Poland; the abbey at Monte Cassino was bombed to smithereens; Admiral Nimitz attacked Turk Island; I organized a cavalcade and toured around in southern Georgia propagandizing the WAC, sometimes covering as many miles in a day as Forrest's cavalry, but with considerably less success. Meanwhile, I was nearing the end of *The Guermantes Way*. In one of my segregated theaters I saw a movie short publicizing the Air Force's OCS. It included a brief shot of John Carroll, beautifully tailored, conferring on a palm-shaded patio with the general to whom he was now an aide. Wormwood! My own General was declared dead a year after his disappearance over Kiel, but I had given him up long before. It was that other Forrest who was alive for me now, for war which had denied the great-grandson a chance had made the great-grandfather an immortal.

This being the case, it was fortunate that in the spring of 1944 I was dispatched to the Special Service School at Washington and Lee University in Lexington, Virginia. In one sense I was moving still further from the Western Theater of the Civil War, but in a more important sense I was getting closer to it than ever. For Lexington was the shrine of Robert E. Lee and Stonewall Jackson, who meant Civil War; and to me wherever there was Civil War, there was above all others Nathan Bedford Forrest. Lee, who had once been superintendent at West Point, was president of Washington and Lee (then simply Washington College) during the few years that remained to him after the war. In mid-September of 1865, he arrived at Lexington astride his faithful battle companion, Traveller, after a lonely three-day ride through the late summer heat of the Blue Ridge mountains. As president, his compensation was $1500 a year, plus one-fifth of the tuition fees, plus the house in the dining room of which he ultimately died. Despite his five years at the school, his last words were military, not academic. "Strike the tent," he is reported to have said.

There in the sweet Blue Ridge spring I roomed with another veteran of heroic combat, Johnny Baker, the former All-American guard from the University of Southern California who in 1931 had kicked an historic field goal to defeat Notre Dame 16-14. The program at the school was quite physical, though by OCS standards relaxed and even idyllic. I went often to the chapel to visit the Lee museum, where the memorabilia were, and to stand contemplating the famous recumbent statue of the General. Lee had never met Forrest, but when he was asked who under his command was the greatest soldier, he answered, "A man I have never seen, sir. His name is Forrest." Lying there he looked patriarchal and Jovian— the very model of an old-fashioned college president, a grand loser but hardly a great warrior. I measured him against the portrait of Forrest that I carried in my head and found him wanting. Imagine Forrest going through the war with one horse! I put Lee in a class with my grandfather; at heart he was a peace-loving man who, if he had been young enough when the war was over and all the Southern girls had stopped cheering, might have gone to the real West to homestead and build railroads as my grandfather did (Indian arrows whizzed past his ears while he laid track in the Dakotas, my father told us).

But with Stonewall Jackson it was another matter. His memorabilia were enshrined at Virginia Military Institute, whose campus adjoined that of Washington and Lee. We used the VMI pool for water safety training, but there was no opportunity to view the memorabilia. In 1851, after service in the Mexican War, Jackson came to VMI as professor of natural and experimental philosophy and military tactics, an unlikely combination even in these interdisciplinary times. He got $1200 a year and quarters, fair enough except that he wasn't much of a teacher. He was there ten years, then the war came; in two more years he went from major to lieutenant general and became Stonewall Jackson—"old Jack." War made him as it made Sherman and Forrest, then it spitefully unmade him: saw to it that he was killed by moonlight with a stray bullet from his own ranks. Dead in his glory at thirty-nine, he was younger than Forrest had been when he enlisted as a private.

Like Forrest, too, Jackson's beginnings had been inauspicious. He was four when his lawyer father died almost destitute, seven when his mother died. An uncle raised him in the Ohio Valley, where he got the usual haphazard schooling and for a short time was a school teacher himself. One of his pupils, his uncle's slave, learned so well that he was able to write himself a pass and escape through the underground railroad. As a military leader, he was, like Forrest, the sternest of disciplinarians; temperamentally, as General Grant said of him, he was "a man of the Cromwell stamp, a Puritan" (though unlike Forrest he was never to be featured in a twentieth-century whiskey ad). War for him, says his biographer Lenoir Chambers, "was an inner fire, a secret stimulus, an internal generating power . . ." It "increased his mental activity . . . endowed him with new energy . . . stirred his imagination." The war to him, as to Forrest, was a holy crusade to which he devoted himself utterly; that God was on his side he never doubted. He too was a superb tactician, a master of the use of propaganda and surprise.

Jackson is buried in the Confederate cemetery at Lexington. I went there twice in early evening, once with Johnny Baker, once alone. Then in midspring it was lushly unkempt, a melancholy land of the dead, a wound that nature was trying to heal by overgrowing it. Allen Tate's "Ode to the Confederate Dead," with its sense of aching yet glamorous futility, catches the very spirit of it. It occurred to me that Tate might have had this very cemetery in mind, especially since Jackson is the only person he mentions:

> Stonewall, Stonewall—and the sunken fields of
> hemp. Shiloh, Antietam, Malvern Hill, Bull Run . . .

In any event, it has ever since been Forrest's poem for me, not Jackson's. After all, Shiloh is there, and Forrest was at Shiloh, and so was Sherman (but not my grandfather; it was too early for him). The *beau sabreur* came close to being killed at Shiloh: was shot in the hip at close range, and again lost a horse. Jackson is buried in the middle of the cemetery, surrounded by his colonels, losers all, like my old guards. Some of the graves had fallen in blackly, as if they were ragged entrances to a macabre underworld. It is easy to imagine Bela Lugosi rising out of there by moonlight to go lusting after the blood of the Blue Ridge virgins.

Jackson made it possible to bring Forrest into another and unanticipated association. In late November of 1859, the former took an artillery detachment of VMI cadets to Charleston as security forces at the hanging of John Brown. He was struck with Brown's "unflinching firmness" as he rode on his coffin to the place of execution; he, the strict Presbyterian and former Sunday school teacher, hoped that Brown was prepared to die but had his doubts, since the condemned man had refused to have a minister the night before. What he could not have realized was the extent to which Brown was the ideal type of that class of men to which he himself, Forrest, and Sherman belonged (to say nothing of Vince Lombardi). All of them were fanatics and war-lovers, but none of them to the degree that Brown was: with his hyperbole Brown defines them all.

Forrest and Brown would have hated each other—the one a former slave trader who would in time be an early leader of the KKK, the other the passionate abolition-ist who hoped that Harper's Ferry would be the spark that would set the slave-holding South ablaze. Yet how alike they were otherwise: the same lowly beginnings and deprivations of early childhood, the same painful loss of parents and early assumption of man's estate, the same intense Puritan personalities. In their pictures there is even the same fierce and ominous concentration of purpose. And Brown had his Pottawatomie Massacre to put alongside Forrest's Fort Pillow. Brown once said to Emerson that he believed in two things, the Bible and the Declaration of Independence, and that it was "better that a whole generation of men, women and children should pass away by violent death than that a word of either should be violated in this country." Forrest—at least the Forrest of the war years—would have understood this.

Such people do not serve causes the way most of us do. Causes intoxicate them; perhaps that is why, like Forrest and Brown, they have so little need for literal intoxicants (Forrest said that he let his staff do his drinking for him). For them,

people do not exist in their own right; they exist to the end of grand causes in which
the fanatic war-lovers (they are always war-lovers) are so intensely alive. You can hear
something of their belligerent zest in the words with which the transcendental
Emerson greeted the outbreak of hostilities: "Ah! sometimes gunpowder smells
good." The Southern diarist Mary James Chestnut might have been speaking of all
of them when she said of Jackson: "He did not value human life when he had an
object to accomplish." And Thoreau, the pacifist-abolitionist who wanted Brown to
hang, "doubting if a prolonged life, if any life, can do as much good as his death"—
what is he but a fanatic war-lover too? There was something of this fanatic temper in
Sherman as well, despite the cavalier strains in him and despite a deficiency of the
religious zeal that inspired Forrest, Jackson, and Brown. He was "akin to the Old
Testament prophet and law-giver," says B. H. Liddell-Hart, his biographer. "The
land must be purified by fire; and in this purification he would bear the torch."
How appropriate then that he marched out of burning Atlanta with his band
playing "John Brown's soul goes marching on." Even Walt Whitman, who as a
hospital missionary ultimately took Southern soldiers under his wing, was wrought
up enough after the first battle of Bull Run to chant:

> Make no parley—stop for no expostulation,
> Mind not the timid—mind not the weeper or prayer,
> Mind not the old man beseeching the young man,
> Let not the child's voice be heard, nor the mother's entreaties,
> Make even the trestles to shake the dead where they lie awaiting
> the hearses . . .

Is it any wonder then that the Civil War was so bloody?

Some people, fortunately, have little of this frantic ferocity: Frederick Douglass,
the great black leader, for instance, who wanted no part of Brown's Harper's Ferry
business; Robert E. Lee (perhaps it was why Traveller was still alive at the end of the
war); General Sooy Smith, in Sherman's view a second-rater whom he damned with
faint praise as "a most accomplished gentleman and a skillful engineer"; Forrest's
great-grandson (or was it there in embryo waiting for the nurturing conditions he
did not survive to experience?); my grandfather, who nevertheless helped Sherman
bear the torch; my bungling guards, *les hommes moyens sensuels*, who, though
intoxicated by no grand schemes, would nevertheless go through life enthralled by

imaginary black panthers.

But give Forrest credit: he was not as thoroughly the God-and-cause-intoxicated man that Brown was. In war he was a reckless enough daredevil, but there was a point beyond which (at Shiloh and Selma, for instance) he would not needlessly endanger his men. People existed for him as people to an extent that they did not for Jackson or Brown, for the latter of whom even slaves belonged to the Cause before they belonged to themselves. I find it easy to believe that Forrest was less responsible for the massacre at Fort Pillow than Brown for the one at Pottawatomie, though Forrest had been a slave-holder and Brown was (as he himself never doubted) on the side of the angels. When the South had surrendered, some of Forrest's men wanted him to lead them across the Mississippi in order to continue the struggle, but Forrest immediately saw the folly of this. He may have been a *beau sabreur*, but he was no Don Quixote. In his farewell address to his troops, he said: "Reason dictates and humanity demands that no more blood be shed." He went back to his plantation and, like my grandfather, became for a while a railroad builder. In 1869, being then Grand Wizard, he officially disbanded the Klan because it had become dangerously violent. In time he was even able to apologize to avoid killing a man in a duel. Towards the end, says Wyeth, an old friend observed in him "a softness of expression and mildness of manner which he had not noticed in the trying times of war." Could Brown have come to such an end?

V

I left Lexington with a sense of having located General Forrest among his fellow immortals. Back then to the mundane, segregated world of south Georgia: to WAC recruiting, to movie theater management, to USO shows, to watermelon parties and service club dances. Halfway around the globe in either direction, the war proceeded according to the premises laid down for it. Rome fell to the Allies, D-Day arrived, B-29's bombed southern Japan, Patton (a man cut out of Forrest's mold) drove his Third Army across the Marne. I was three quarters of the way through *Remembrance of Things Past* and beginning to wonder if it would last out the war. It did not. I was transferred to the Air Transport Command and shipped to British Guiana. There in the steaming Demarara jungles, not long before V-E Day, I came to the end of Proust—if anyone can be said to have come to the end of a man just as fanatically enthralled by his memory as Forrest and Brown had been by their grand themes. V-J Day arrived; we celebrated half the night and woke with tropical hangovers, which are the worst kind. I became troop commander with nominal power over a thousand or so aircraft maintenance troops, most of whom had never seen me and all of whom wanted to go home at once.

One night before payday I sat in the orderly room beside my young Tennessee first sergeant, the effective troop commander whom I always felt guilty not saluting and whose respect I was able to keep only by beating him at ping pong. On the table in front of us were pay envelopes, pay records, two canvas bags containing many thousands of dollars in flamboyant British Guianese paper money and British coins, and our loaded 45's. In the jungle beyond the barracks area, a quarter of a mile away in the fetid heart of darkness, were snakes of all descriptions, sleeping macaws and toucans, mosquitoes loaded with malaria and filaria, voodoo, native girls with exotic venereal diseases, and, if one had the courage to go looking for them, real black panthers. None of this menaced us, however; the 45's were for official decoration only. We worked late into the night, stuffing the pay envelopes. It came to me suddenly that the war was really over, that like Lee and my grandfather I had survived. I knew then with premonitory hindsight that if I actually had become General Forrest's aide, I would not have survived. Sooner or later, given his capabilities and the tradition behind him, he would have gotten me to where the real action was and where generals' aides would have been as expendable as his great-grandfather's horses. With him, my future would have been a succession of Kiels, one of which would certainly have done me in.

One day after the war, I learned the address of Forrest's residence during his Spokane years, before he departed with the secret orders that turned out to be orders for death. I went looking for it, remembering the neighborhood as one noted for its graceful old three- and four-story mansions and hoping to discover that he had lived in one of these so that my memory of both Forrests would be as firmly anchored in space and time as Proust's memory had been by his madeleine and tea. No building whatever existed at this address; a mammoth parking lot had consumed the entire area. Fate that had given him a running start had not only tripped him up but had finally covered him with concrete.

Perhaps I expected too much. Why should fate have treated the General more tenderly than my grandfather, whom Sherman did not bother to mention in his *Memoirs*? Still it was another shock to discover that when General Hap Arnold's autobiography *Global Mission* appeared in 1949 there was no reference to Forrest in it, despite the fact that everyone else of any consequence in the history of the Air

Force was mentioned. Clearly, his mistake was not to have survived long enough. To enter history, it is not enough merely to survive; unless one survives beyond a certain point—and for everyone the point is different—one has no chance at all. Thus the first General Forrest, who like Jackson, Brown, Sherman, Lee, and Lee's horse did not make that mistake, is on record for the ages, while his great-grandson must be content to exist alongside the hanged novelist and my grandfather's cheering Southern girls as simply another thread in the seamless web of one man's past.

That First Postwar Season
1945 - 1946

P alm Beach for me is always associated with a full-page Helena Rubinstein ad that appeared in the January, 1946, *Social Spectator*, a copy of which I picked up somewhere on Worth Avenue at a time when I was enjoying an outsider-insider's relationship with that fabulous island. The ad in question was titled "Triumph over Time," and the reference was to estrogenic hormone cream and oil, the magical or imaginary properties of which products, especially as administered in Miss Rubinstein's Worth Avenue salon, guaranteed a "high-hearted disregard for time." The heroine of the ad was an exquisitely coifed and ermined woman whose heart could not have been higher and for whom time had clearly ceased to be a problem. Bemused as I was with the place, I saw her as a symbolic figure whose real reference was to the island itself. So transposed, the ad ceased to be hyperbolic.

The first great post-war season was over when I left Palm Beach for the second and last time, but I was still half convinced that in that transposed ad lay the key to the meaning of Palm Beach: that in some real way it did triumph over time, so that if certain individuals could not rise to its promise it was because they had failed Palm Beach, not it them. By then I had seen the island in contexts that sometimes troubled me; nevertheless, I returned from it to a world of accelerating change with a sense of having left behind something that would not change, much as Hugh Conway in James Hilton's *Lost Horizon* leaves Shangri-la. It would continue to be free of billboards, slums, smog, Taco stands, used car lots, neon signs, supermarkets and intemperate weather. Should the crass world prove too menacing, it could always pull up its three drawbridges and isolate its virtue—as indeed its mayor threatened to do not so long ago when Negroes were rioting a hundred miles to the north.

In time, of course, I learned that Palm Beach really had changed in certain respects. Condominium apartments had sprung up at the east end of Worth Avenue and elsewhere; the public beach had deteriorated; dream palaces like E. T. Stokesbury's El Mirasol and Mrs. Horace Dodge's Playa Riente had disappeared; a par three golf course had been built at the south end where I could remember nothing but sand dunes and wind-tortured palm trees; some of the more energetic matrons had gone into trade; the recession had made bargain-shopping in West Palm Beach fashionable; there was even a supermarket on Palm Beach itself, architecturally cosmeticized, however, so as not to disturb the spirit of founding father Addison Mizner. Perhaps even more consequential, if one was to believe a Niven Busch article in *Holiday,* was the appearance of a new-swinging vital Enclave that had combined with a new-rich Netherworld to revitalize a stuffy, tradition-bound society. Of course, it is possible to believe that none of these changes has gotten to the heart of the matter, that indeed no conceivable changes could. After all, one of Palm Beach's most knowledgeable and powerful senior citizens, Mrs. Stephen Stanford, was able to say only a year ago that "it's exactly the same as when I came here in 1933."

I arrived there somewhat later myself, in early July of 1945 on my way to an Air Transport Command assignment in British Guiana, a place where, from an American point of view, time, far from having been triumphed over, had not even started. My first view of Palm Beach was a Keatsian one from the Comeau building in West Palm Beach, where the ATC's Caribbean Division had wisely located its headquarters. As I looked eastward from the seventh floor, Palm Beach was so exquisitely set between Lake Worth and the impossibly blue Atlantic that it

> Charm'd magic casements, opening on the foam
> Of perilous seas in faery lands forlorn,

As soon as I could get away I rented a bicycle and crossed over on Flagler Memorial Bridge, knowing no more about Flagler, or the reasons for his memorialization, than I knew about Helena Rubinstein. I turned south on Lake Trail, pedaled through a Hollywood-style jungle and discovered the abandoned Whitehall; crossed the island eastward on Pine Walk with the browned-over fairways of the Palm Beach Golf Club on both sides of me; arrived at The Breakers, parked the bike and prowled about. I had seen no one; everything was closed, boarded up, shuttered, posted against trespassers. Debris had blown into the corners of the great rampart on the sea side of the hotel. Furniture could be seen stacked and covered in the glassed-in lounge. The hotel and grounds had a petrified sumptuousness, as if all life had been arrested there at the point of intensest realization. The waiting soundlessness of the scene was emphasized by the crash of surf on the sea-littered beach. I might have stumbled on the remains of an ancient high civilization in an Andean jungle.

But eventually, as I was leaving along the east end of the golf course, I did meet someone: a garrulous and biscuit-brown watchman who seemed to be as glad as I was to meet another human being amidst all that lonesome grandeur. He biked around the premises four times nightly, he said, but encountered no prowlers or vandals. It was an easy job though monotonous. He longed for the winter season to start in December, when every night would be like a picnic. He urged me to return then, though he must have seen that I was not to that manor born. I said that I would like very much to do so and thanked him for the invitation. I left him and pedaled over to that avenue of kings, Royal Poinciana Way, then with mixed emotions left that enclave in time for the middle class vitality of West Palm Beach. I intended to return the next day for further explorations, but the orders for British Guiana had come, so I went to another enclave in time that did not know it was waiting for Cheddi Jagan to drag it violently into the twentieth century.

Before very many months had passed, the atom bombs were dropped on Japan, the war was declared officially over, and I was recalled to headquarters in West Palm Beach to help preside over the ATC's collapsing empire. So now in October I was back on the seventh floor of the Comeau building with its superb view of the magic island that I had never expected to see again. I found a shop where for seventy dollars a man built me a bike out of accumulated odds and ends (new bikes were still as scarce as scotch whiskey). The man said I might think of his creation as a Schwinn since its parts were more Schwinn than anything else; actually, it looked and was completely anonymous. For a few extra dollars I got a battery-run lamp, a wicker basket to strap in front of the handlebars, and a combination lock. Now I had all the transportation anyone needed, night or day, to enjoy Palm Beach; indeed, it was often the only kind of transportation available even to displaced European aristocrats. Thus I was able to resume my love affair with Palm Beach not only with ease but with style. For the "real" pre-war or black market bikes of the wealthy had a production line sameness about them, whereas mine was immediately recognized as a custom-made original.

The golf courses had greened up now, a few luxury craft were moored in Yacht

Harbor, there were signs of life on Worth Avenue, but the season had not yet started. It was an ideal time to explore the place, which I began to do on late afternoons and weekends. I became familiar with every drive, court, trail, walk and lane, and worked them into a variety of tour combinations. Best of all was the Grand Tour, of which I never tired. I went over to Flagler Bridge; turned south on Lake Trail (once the speedway for dowagers in afromobiles); continued on it past Whitehall to the intersection at Royal Palm Way; then along Lake Drive so that I could pass by the Municipal Pier and Yacht Harbor to check on new arrivals; east then on Worth Avenue and south on County Road with Everglades golf course on my right and the roar of the not yet visible ocean to the left in my ears; then east on El Bravo to the sudden immense blue of the Gulfstream with its purple band at the horizon above which the ice-blue thunderheads boiled; then north along Ocean Boulevard taking in what the scene offered: the red water over the rock reefs, sandpipers skittering away from the lacy clawing surf, pelicans diving shoulder-deep for fish, sunbathers and swimmers strewn brightly over the public beach, a few affluent idlers lounging against the colored windbreaks of the Seaspray Beach Club, a rusty-prowed tramp steamer close in to avoid the tug of the Gulfstream; then west to the County Road to get around The Breakers and the golf course; then back to the ocean at Sunset Avenue; then left on Wells Road to County Road and so north to the Lake Worth Inlet, where I might see a fishing launch come in from the sea, bucking the rough water of the inlet, with triumphant white flag up and the tail of a sailfish or two showing above the stern railing; then back south on County Road all the way to Royal Palm Way, ideally at five o'clock so that I could hear the chimes sound sweetly over the island from Bethesda-by-the-Sea; and so home to West Palm Beach reality by way of South Bridge.

Another kind of tour covered much less territory, but it afforded a view of the place unavailable to a biker. An officer friend who had a pre-war knowledge of Palm Beach would lead me on twilight prowls around the still deserted mansions and cottages. Since he knew of little-used or forgotten gates and stiles, clandestine passages through and around hedges and almost invisible interconnecting jungle trails, I was able to experience such places as the J. P. Kennedy and Claude Boettcher estates, Sandreef, El Mirasol and Playa Riente from angles that would have been strange to their owners. Twilight and early dusk gave these pleasure places an eerie glamour. Once in the gathering darkness, we squeezed through a hedge and found ourselves beside an empty and, as it seemed in the crepuscular light, frighteningly deep swimming pool that my friend had forgotten was there. One had to take it on faith that life would return to that place.

But life did return, not with a bang but the way spring returns, bud by bud and leaf by leaf: more and more lights in Whitehall, The Breakers, the Palm Beach Hotel and The Villas; more and bigger yachts in Yacht Harbor and at Municipal Pier; more and more lovely tanned legs pumping bikes on Worth Avenue; more and more loungers against the windbreaks at the Seaspray Beach Club; more and more listeners to the Saturday morning opera broadcasts in the Four Arts reading room; more and more golfers roaming the Palm Beach Golf Club between Whitehall and The Breakers (occasionally someone's wild drive came with grand kangaroo leaps down County Road). Palm Beach, observed a lady reporter in the *Social Spectator,* was emerging from its wartime somberness "like a gay, lovely butterfly casting off its cocoon-like shell to soar aloft in the tropical sunshine."

Soon my friend's aunt, an American-born countess, arrived to open her medium-sized mansion for the season, and I became part of her entourage. Thus my career as bedazzled outsider was pleasantly modified. I appeared at a variety of social functions, sometimes as spear holder, sometimes as general utility man, less often as full scale participant. We went to dinner at Tab-oo and the Everglades Club, to the horse races at Gulfstream, the dog races at West Palm Beach, and the symphony concerts at the Paramount theater. One evening while others played bridge, I spent three hours playing backgammon with a teen-age French heiress who looked like Hedy Lamar but was almost completely mindless. On another occasion I spent most of an evening listening to an English-educated Italian woman describe all her favorite scenes from Red Skelton's *A Confederate Yankee,* which I had the tact to pretend I had not seen.

There was much talk about *Oklahoma!* and *Harvey,* about the hardships of the war years, about the peaceful use of atomic energy, and about the scarcity of servants and such necessary luxuries as eatable meat and drinkable whisky (I experienced no shortage of either so long as I stayed on the east side of Lake Worth). I became familiar with a baron from the lowlands who was bored with all these subjects and wanted to discuss the history of the English language, about which he seemed to know more than I did, even though I had taught the course several times. Sometimes I met his American-born baroness between five and six o'clock as I biked along Lake Trail, the great pockets of her ankle-length skirt bulging with oranges she had filched as she strolled along the trail. As I leaned on the handlebars chatting with her, the late afternoon sun glanced off the gently lapping lake and shimmered on the palm fronds above us.

Many of the headquarters officers were absorbed into the social life of the island. Most of them were more legitimately there than I was: the upper echelons of the Air Transport Command were notoriously full of well-connected people, a fact that helped to account for the relaxed, country-club atmosphere of the Comeau building. But whether they were kissing cousins to natives or merely spear-holders and general utility men as I was, they were welcome and in demand. Nothing is better than being an officer in a resort area at the end of a popular and victorious war that at one time seemed endless and to which everyone has had at least the illusion of being seriously committed. Then the uniform cuts across all social barriers, the way clerical garb did in the middle ages, camouflaging both the snobbery of the rich and the snobbery of the temporarily elevated poor. For the moment duke and peasant are men of the world together over their martinis as they enjoy a democracy they will not experience again till they are in their graves. Without my uniform and my captain's bars (it was advisable to be at least a captain), I couldn't have played backgammon with the beautiful French heiress, nor gone dinner dancing at the Everglades, nor gossiped about Grimm's Law with the Baron.

But the officer's uniform was at least as good for Palm Beach as it was for its wearers. By giving a patriotic spice to the general euphoria, it helped to make the first grand post-war season a national celebration. The uniform was a reminder that Palm Beach, like Lucky Strike green, had in its own way gone to war. It had endured the threat of German submarine invasions; it had turned the Palm Beach Biltmore and the Sea and Surf Club over to the Navy; its Volunteers for Victory had among other things run a canteen and an enlisted men's bath house; in midwar its Everglades Club had set some kind of record entertaining 9200 enlisted men at a Christmas party. Besides, any uniform reinforced (and was reinforced by) the native sons themselves who were back in full regalia: lieutenant commanders and colonels, here and there a Pentagon brigadier or rear admiral, gorgeous from their dress uniforms and modest fruit salads.

If Niven Busch's distinctions between Enclave and Netherworld, between established rich and upstart rich, obtained, then my uniform kept me from being aware of them. C. A. Munn's famous Christmas list of the 150 most important people must have come into being much later as part of an effort to raise the drawbridges against the threat of the Visigoths; certainly such a list would have violated the ecumenical spirit of that season. I noted in the *Social Spectator* that the Surfside Hotel advertised itself not only as having character but as "restricted," and I did sometimes hear a restricted remark from one of the natives, but it usually came across to me (especially in the early weeks of the season) as reflexive rather than rancorous, like an obscenity muttered over a missed putt. Besides, in that unrestricted atmosphere it was easy to believe that the Surfside simply did not want the business of rowdies and unmarried couples.

In any event, the more striking thing at the time was that the great ones of the earth were there, and it seemed quite natural that I was among them. As I consult my records now I find, among many others: the Prince and Princess Alexis Zalstem-Zalesky (she the Johnson and Johnson bandaid heiress), Mr. and Mrs. Stuyvesant Pierrepont, Princess Constance Pignatelli, Mr. and Mrs. Robert R. Young (he the famous railroad tycoon), the fashion-setter Arthur Bradley Campbell, the man-about-town Captain Alastair Mackintosh, Sir Leslie Hore-Belisha (famous for having become British Minister of War after having distinguished himself in Flanders and at Salonika in World War I), and of course the brothers Munn, C. A. and Gurnee (famous for their profitable connection with pari-mutuel machines). Joseph P. Kennedy arrived with his wife, his daughter the Marchioness of Hartington, and his son, Lieutenant John, whose time, like Cheddi Jagan's, was still to come. General Jonathan Wainright, the hero of Corregidor, and Vincent Sheehan lectured for the Palm Beach Round Table, Carl Sandburg and Ely Culbertson for the Four Arts (in the Comeau building I lectured to enlisted men on the wisdom of using the G.I. bill to attend college). The USS *Sequoia* tied up at the John S. Phipps' Lake Worth Dock, and Navy Secretary James Forrestal came down to join it. Postmaster Robert Hannegan was said to be pursuing sailfish out in the Gulfstream. In a bar on Worth Avenue I heard one man say casually to another that he had been playing golf with the Duke of Windsor. Count Maurice Maeterlinck, Nobel laureate and author of *The Bluebird*, was somebody's guest in the neighborhood of the Everglades Club. Igor Gorin, Sir Thomas and Lady Beecham all appeared in concert at the Paramount theater (at the Beecham affair I sat a few rows ahead of Sumner Wells, the former undersecretary of State). *Life* magazine caught the great baritone Lawrence Tibbet on the beach at Sandreef in swimming trunks and standing on his head for an admiring audience that included the Princess Zalstem-Zalesky and the Marchioness of Hartington.

Naturally, I saw few of these people and met still fewer of them (though I was there in spirit when Lawrence Tibbet stood on his head, for I knew Sandreef well from my twilight prowlings). Nevertheless, thanks to the magic of my uniform, I had the sense of being eligible, and even likely, to meet any one of them at any moment, even C. A. Munn himself, and to talk with him or her as easily as I talked with the Baron about Grimm's law.

But the grandest of all collections of notables, the most glamorous and glittering of the season's rituals, was the great New Years' Eve party at the Everglades—"one of the loveliest places in all this world," as a lady society reporter called it. I heard later that gala times were had elsewhere that night at the Patio, the Sailfish Club, the South Ocean Club, and The Breakers, but they must have been makeshift affairs for those who couldn't get reservations at the Everglades, which closed a week earlier than usual. My party arrived in the midst of the festivities, having first dined on squab at Tab-oo. Surely never before or since has there been such a high-hearted disregard for time. The club was embarking on the second quarter century of its illustrious existence with a program that included backgammon on Tuesday evenings and gin rummy on Saturday evenings, but that night, as one moved among the euphoric throngs in the central lounge, the dining room, the Gray Room, and the bar, the general expectation seemed to be that of a Golden Age for all the world. I danced in the Orange Gardens to the music of Maynard Rutherford's orchestra with two French girls—princesses, I was told by the Countess—whose hawk-nosed patrician father resembled the novelist François Mauriac. They were lovely slender girls with exotic accents. I kissed them both at midnight after the singing of Auld Lang Syne. Everybody in fact kissed everybody in a grand communal triumph over time.

But life was really more complicated than this. All along I had been living in a West Palm Beach hotel on Datura street just around the corner from the Comeau building. It was an ancient three-story wooden structure from which the paint had weathered away. It catered to elderly retired people and pensioners, mainly widows, many of whom lived there the year round because the rates even during the winter season were low and all the amenities of life were available within easy walking distance at prices they could afford. I was there for the same reasons; therefore when it got through to me that I was the only person under sixty among the guests and that the place was really in an appalling state of decay, I could not bring myself to move.

But as I came to see more clearly later, my attachment to it transcended

economy and convenience. The hotel intensified by contrast the experience of Palm
Beach. Instead of shopping at Fuller's or Slater's on Worth Avenue, its guests
shopped at Lerner's or Woolworth's on Clematis street in West Palm Beach; instead
of eating squab at Tab-oo or The Alibi, they ate fillet of sole or Salisbury steak at
one of the cheap cafés on Clematis or Datura, or perhaps, on the few occasions
when they could afford to celebrate, at the George Washington or Pennsylvania
hotels; instead of backgammon and golf at the Everglades Club, they played checkers
and shuffleboard at Flagler Park; instead of listening to grand opera in the Four Arts
reading room, they gathered in the small cheaply furnished lobby for the communal
experience of Fibber McGee and Molly and Jack Benny; instead of lolling on the
sand at the Seaspray Club, where they could see the fishing boats out in the
Gulfstream, they sat on a bench below Flagler Park and watched the ferry cross over
from Palm Beach. They read movie magazines, not the *Social Spectator*; they went to
movies at the Florida theater, not the Paramount; they did not talk about *Harvey* or
Oklahoma! or the Duke of Windsor's golf or the comings and goings of the Princess
Zalstem-Zalesky. They talked about their aches and pains, about their departed wives
or husbands, about their unvisiting children who were far away in the frozen north,
and about Fibber McGee and Jack Benny. No doubt, when they could not distract
themselves with other subjects, they worried about money. The women did not use
Helena Rubinstein's estrogenic hormone cream; they bought their cosmetics at
Woolworth's, used them too lavishly and dyed their hair garishly. The men did not
dress like Arthur Bradley Campbell and the women did not dress like Mrs.
Harrison Williams. Their attitude toward time was anything but one of high-hearted
disregard; time was all too obviously triumphing over them.

The contrast was especially striking at night, when I would return late to my
pathetic hotel from an evening of fine food and liquor, music and dancing in the
company of well-turned-out and well-heeled people in that enclave out of time. There
would be one dim light on the creaky verandah, the manager would have gone to
bed, the lobby would be deserted, the corridors would smell of old people and
cheap perfume. Snores, stifled cries and arthritic groans would come from behind
closed doors. I would imagine the old people hugging their lives desperately, hearing
time coming with their sharp ears, some of them afraid to sleep for fear of being
taken unawares; for sometimes, much to the manager's irritation, they died in their
rooms, having no place else to die.

Soon I began to perform the same utility-man functions in the hotel that I was performing on the other side of Lake Worth. The old people were obviously proud, if a little surprised, to have a young officer among them and liked to have me do small favors. I moved lobby chairs, picked up shawls, adjusted the lobby radio, gave an arm to rheumatic grandmothers I met on the stairs (the place had no elevator). My most important chore was to repair the electrical system. The hotel, like most buildings in southern Florida, had no defense against sudden nocturnal drops in temperature. The old people would immediately turn on their electric heaters (as vital to them as oxygen to a diver) and fail to turn off their radios; the fuses would blow, and the manager would come looking for me with his flashlight. He claimed to be unable to detect a blown fuse even with his glasses on, but he was really afraid, with good reason, to reach into the chaotically wired fuse box. So I would go with him as if following an usherette down a theater aisle to the dark corner of the second floor corridor where the fuse box was, the old people standing intensely silent in their doorways like ghosts momentarily reprieved from their tombs. After all, it was an event that broke the monotony of their lives in a most personal way: there was always the possibility that the current would not come on again and the cold would seep like death into their bones. After I had replaced the blown fuse, the manager would lecture his pin-curled and weirdly kimonoed guests about the importance of not overloading the circuit, and they would retreat silently into their room-tombs.

But in time, as I shuttled back and forth between these two worlds, the hotel became less a defining contrast with Palm Beach and more a continuation of it in reduced terms. This was partially because, except for events like the great New Year's Eve party, my Palm Beach associates tended more and more to be old people, especially women I was expected to amuse and cater to. At cocktail parties I was invariably stuck with one of them; often I had one on each side at dinner. They had the advantage of Helena Rubinstein and may even have eaten estrogenic hormone cream like caviar, but they had long ago ceased to treat time with high-handed disregard; two manhattans made them mawkish; they could no longer eat with relish, not even squab. Perhaps they were on first-name basis with the Princess Alexis Zalstem-Zalesky, had had full vision of Arthur Bradley Campbell in his beautiful clothes, and had once danced till dawn in the Orange Room, but their consciousnesses had not been raised perceptibly. They would not have known who Maeterlinck was. If they talked about *Oklahoma!* or *Harvey*, they were no more interesting to listen to than were their counterparts across the lake when they talked

about Fibber McGee, and they were if anything more likely to have restricted ideas.
And they seemed just as afraid that burnt-out fuses would prove irreplaceable.

The perception of such continuities did not spoil Palm Beach for me but it did
qualify my pleasure in it, just as did my growing awareness that the *Social Spectator*
was really a movie magazine in disguise. I began to think of writing a novel that
would relate these two apparently disparate worlds in some significant way. I took
many notes, gathered documents, did much preliminary scribbling in a notebook,
toyed with various approaches and arrangements of material. When I returned to
my hotel room at dawn New Year's morning, having kissed the French princesses at
midnight in the Orange Room, I had the sense of being able to bring the project off
effortlessly. Perhaps I had really seen, if only vaguely, the one true way into the
subject. In any event it was no longer visible when I woke up badly hung over some
hours later.

Meanwhile the Palm Beach season and the Air Transport Command wound
down together. Headquarters was moved from the Comeau building to Morrison
Field. I gave up my hotel room and moved to quarters on the base. The Countess
departed and, of necessity, I reverted to my outsider's relationship with Palm Beach.
I went two or three more times to the public beach, but it was really too far for the
bike. There was no more golf at the Everglades and no more real rubber pre-war golf
balls, which we had been able to buy from the Black caddies, who used ladders to
salvage them from crew-cut palm trees that lined the superb fairways. Instead we
climbed over a fence behind the base and carried our Special Service clubs and
synthetic golf balls across country to the first tee of the Belvedere Country Club, a
place over which time in the form of wartime neglect had triumphed.

When I left Morrison Field for the Pacific Northwest, Palm Beach had returned
to its off-season hibernation. By then the bike had become too symbolically involved
with the place to be sold or abandoned. I shipped it home, though the Florida East
Coast freight agent warned me to expect the worst. When it finally arrived somewhat battered, I had been a civilian for many weeks. I hammered it back into shape
and returned to my weekend tours. Thus, despite the substitution of buttercup and
pine tree for bougainvillea and date palm, I was able for a while to revive Palm
Beach sensations. But the bike which in Palm Beach had seemed to me so distinctive was now simply freakish. One Sunday afternoon I passed a convoy of my
students on their new postwar bikes. There was no mistaking the quality of the
amusement on their faces: they were scratching me off their C. A. Munn lists. That

evening I put the bike in the garage and never rode it again. Some years later, in a lean time, I advertised it in the Sunday paper and sold it for twelve dollars.

It is long gone now. But so is Count Maurice Maeterlinck, having, one hopes, made his blue bird stand still at last; and Robert R. Young, famous for railroads, who told his wife they were broke and then blew out his brains; and Sir Thomas Beecham, who drew such glorious vitality out of Beethoven's Seventh that night in the Paramount theater; and Sumner Wells with his handsome silver head who sat there in the audience listening; and James Forrestal who may have been there too but who three years later threw himself out of the sixteenth floor of the Bethesda Naval Hospital in Washington, D. C.; and Lawrence Tibbett who stood on his head at Sandreef for the Princess Zalstem-Zalesky and the Marchioness of Hartington; and the Marchioness herself who was so amused; and her brother Lieutenant John, whose time was yet to come and go; and the Duke of Windsor; and Sir Leslie Hore-Belisha who was later to become a baron; and all the old people in the West Palm Beach hotel who were so afraid that the lights would not come on again. Time triumphed over all of them. Not even Helena Rubinstein could go on forever, though it appeared for a while that she might.

Occasionally something would revive the memory of Palm Beach. It might be an act as trivial as putting a bandaid on my daughter's skinned knee, which would remind me of the Princess Zalstem-Zalesky, who because I had never met her continued to be a powerfully evocative symbol. Or it might be news of the death at ninety-four of Helena Rubinstein and the discovery that by grace of her second husband she was the Princess Archil Gourielli-Tchkonia: distressing information, actually, since by making her sound like a character out of an early Marx Brothers movie, it took her out of the mythic world of estrogenic hormone cream. If I had nothing better to work on after such Proustian experiences, I would get out my Palm Beach story and try once more to bring the two worlds together in a meaningful action. Out of much less promising material I eventually wrote another novel that won a prize, but the Palm Beach story remained as dead as Henry Flagler's Royal Poinciana Hotel.

In time I came to see that my problem was the same as Niven Busch's. You do not get the truth about Palm Beach from Niven Busch because he is too much in love with the place; therefore, his irony has no cutting edge. His Palm Beach like mine may be disguised as a place on the map, but it is above all an island of the mind. Everybody has one—Coleridge his Pantisocracy, Yeats his Byzantium, Sir

Walter Ralegh his El Dorado—but not everybody makes the mistake of thinking he has found it somewhere under the sun. Such a place, lying "full of peace and joy" within the soul of man, Melville calls an insular Tahiti, but he warns us in *Moby Dick* that he who pushes off from it will never be able to return because it is encompassed "by all the horrors of the half known life."

I like to think that Count Maeterlinck, who was eighty-four that winter when he stayed in the cottage behind the Everglades Club, knew better than to push off from the island in his mind—which is what he would have done if he had confused it with Palm Beach or any other particular place. Surely he would have expected to find there not his blue bird but only the creature comforts of the unbelievable winter afternoons and evenings, with the music of the not too distant surf in his ears when the wind was right. But once I had let that glamorous sand spit contaminate the island in my mind, I could never be sure which of the two places I was trying to reconcile with the encompassing horrors.

The Guiana Connection
1945

The context of E. M. Forster's famous "Only connect!" in *Howard's End* leaves some readers with the impression that the strenuous job of making vital connections among what would otherwise be disparate fragments is entirely up to them. Fortunately, as Forster himself no doubt knew, some of the most interesting connections are the serendipitous consequences of being in a certain place at a certain time. In my case, if it had not been for a wartime assignment to British Guiana (the last place in the world I would have chosen), Sir Walter Ralegh,[1] Evelyn Waugh, and the Reverend Jim Jones would have remained forever disconnected fragments.

In 1595, the first of three incarcerations in the Tower of London behind him, Sir Walter Ralegh sailed to and explored the northeast coast of South America. He spent most of his time in what we now call Venezuela, but that does not keep his subsequent bestseller, *The Discoverie of the Large, Rich and Bewtiful Empire of Guiana*, from being a proper beginning point for anyone's experience of the Guianas. Evelyn Waugh discovered Guiana during a three-month period beginning in late 1932 and got from the experience two books, *Ninety-two Days* (an account of his travels through British Guiana into northern Brazil) and the brilliant novel (now a brilliant movie), *A Handful of Dust*. Being an Oxford educated Englishman, he

---

1. In this essay all quotations from Ralegh's Discovery of Guiana are from the 1596 edition, as republished now in the Hakluyt series. I have followed the English spelling of Sir Walter's name since it appears to be the one he preferred.

would have known that Ralegh, himself an Oxonian, had preceded him. However, it is not likely that Reverend Jim Jones, first and last messiah of The People's Temple, and an expert in bogus connections, had Ralegh in mind when he first saw British Guiana in 1963 or when he returned there thirteen years later with his band of doomed utopians.

My own discovery of Guiana came between Waugh and Jones at a time when Ralegh was not much on my mind and Waugh himself, no longer a man-at-arms, was safely back in England. In the summer of 1945, on orders from the Caribbean Division of the Air Transport Command, I flew from Miami to Atkinson Field in British Guiana (now Guyana) with the expectation that I would function as Special Service Officer. It was immediately apparent that I was not needed. To make matters worse, I was quartered with a newly arrived Protestant chaplain who was trying to live with his own irrelevance: the Catholic chaplain, everybody's favorite, had cornered the religious market. In the meantime, he had picked up some kind of fungus that had spread to his back, which it was my duty to anoint with salve each night before he went to bed. Under these circumstances I was often as bored as Ralegh was during his first days in the Brick Tower, where he was denied not only Queen's favor but sight of the traffic on the Thames River.

My release came while the chaplain's fungus was still in full flower: I agreed to take on a weekly radio program to be aired Sunday afternoons at Georgetown in the interest of solidifying relations with our allies, the British, whose empire had not yet begun to disintegrate. So I rode the riverboat twenty-five miles downstream to Georgetown, seeing for the first time the great and muddy Demerara, established myself at the Park Hotel (destined thirty years later to be the in-town headquarter for Jim Jones's People's Temple), and made my arrangements with what I took to be the only radio station in town. For the next two months I spent two or three days each weekend discovering Guiana in ways that would have been impossible if I had remained at Atkinson Field—which, like most American bases on foreign soil, was organized to make possible the constant rediscovery of home.

The discovery of Guiana entailed the rediscovery of Waugh's A *Handful of Dust*. When the novel's central figure, Tony Last, disembarked at Georgetown, "the custom sheds were heavy with the reek of sugar and loud with the buzzing of bees," exactly as they were for me. At this point not only had Tony's marriage collapsed but his vision of a "whole Gothic world had come to grief." Like a Renaissance explorer, he had come to Guiana in search of the "Shining, the Many Watered, the

Bright Feathered" City, a transfiguration of his ancestral Hetton, the discovery of which would be the compensation for all other losses. In search of that City, and led by the eccentric Dr. Messinger, he went arduously up the Demerara and on south into Brazil, where he found not the Shining City but the village of the illiterate half-caste, James Todd (played superbly in the movie by Sir Alec Guinness), to whom he spent the rest of his life reading Dickens.

Ralegh too had gone in search of a City, Manoa, in the kingdom called Eldorado, which, he wrote, "for greatnes, for the riches, and for the excellent seate, it farre exceedeth any of the world." After coming back from his first voyage relatively empty-handed, he did not give up on his dream of the Golden City. Sentenced to the Bloody Tower for treason (he went to the trial puffing his pipe), he continued to publicize Guiana. After thirteen years, the king by then being sufficiently hard up to be tempted by visions of New World gold, the Shepherd of the Ocean (as he called himself) was freed for his second and disastrous voyage, from which he returned to the chopping block.

The radio program was a primitive affair. Most of the time I played popular American music, which I interrupted with disk jockey chatter and a three- or four-minute disquisition on some aspect of the Air Transport Command's contribution to the war effort. The station's manager said the response was good, which was easy enough to say since my only serious competition was the afternoon cricket match. Usually I took the night boat back to the base, lounging on deck with a good Havana cigar as we throbbed into that immense heart of darkness. Sometimes candlelight from a native hut winked through the riverside foliage, or cast a Halloween glow on the water if the hut had been stilted up on the bank, and the candlelight combined with the tropical stars to intensify the dark. It was easy to believe then, as it was widely believed on the base, that there was voodoo in the jungle, orgiastic rituals presided over by the garishly costumed priestesses of the powers of darkness. It was the perfect setting for the atheistic and necromancing School of Night to which Ralegh was suspected of belonging. At such times it was easy to understand too how Ralegh could believe that in Guiana there were Amazons, "cruell and bloodthirsty" women, as well as men whose eyes were in their shoulders and whose mouths were in the middle of their breasts.

Nevertheless, it was a pleasant trip unless it rained, which in Guiana country as Ralegh had learned, it might at any moment ("the raines came downe in terrible showers" so that one's only shirt "was thoroughly washt on his body for the most part ten times in one day"). Coming downstream in daylight I found the jungle shoreline endlessly fascinating, especially when it was tormented by the sudden rain squalls, and was never inclined to spend the time reading. Years later, when Waugh's diaries became available, I noted that there were times when the jungle wildness was less than fascinating to him—times when he preferred to lie in his hammock reading Thomas Aquinas or Shakespeare's *Titus Andronicus*. But by then the jungle had become an all too intimate reality for him, whereas I knew it only from a safe distance. Ralegh, a great reader, had a chest of books with him, but what he read out of it I don't know. It's hard to imagine him not taking along the first three books of Edmund Spenser's *Faerie Queene*, especially since the available edition contained not only his beautiful commendatory sonnet but the famous letter to the "Right noble, and Valorous, Sir Walter Raleigh" in which the "dark conceit" of the poem was spelled out. However, there are sections in it, particularly in Canto XII of Book II where the Bower of Bliss gold is a symbol of deceptive sensual display, that are not likely to give comfort to a man in search of a Golden City.

The Demerara is tidal, like Ralegh's Orinoco, and when the boat had to buck the tide the twenty-five-mile trip could take three hours. Learning that an amphibious courier plane sometimes made the trip, I looked up the pilot, an engaging youngster, and arranged to fly with him the next Saturday morning. Thus I was able to discover Guiana from a new perspective, one that made it all too apparent that no one in his right mind would expect to find a fabulous Golden City in it. But when Jim Jones brought his People's Temple to Guiana he was not, as Ralegh and Tony Last were, in search of a City. He would himself build a City, and it would resist the assaults of time, including the inevitable nuclear holocaust. Against his voodoo powers his entranced followers, having been Cityless too long and for the most part, like Tony Last, secular to begin with, would have had no defense. Like secular people everywhere, they would have lost the habit of religion without losing the appetite for it, so that a false prophet could come among them like a fox into a henhouse. That Ralegh had not lost the habit of religion, in spite of all the dark rumors about his unorthodoxy, is apparent enough in his *History of the World*—the masterwork which, as was the case with his friend Spenser's *The Faerie Queene*, he left incomplete.

No one could have been less secular or less distracted by visions of a Shining and Bright Feathered City than the Catholic chaplain, whom I got to know well after the fungus-ridden Protestant chaplain had been invalided back to the States.

On Sundays he managed to say mass in the French, Dutch, and British Guianas, so that it was one o'clock in the afternoon before he had his first meal of the day. He was actively concerned with the welfare of natives who worked on the base, and he had taken under his wing a leper colony on the Essequibo River. About his own discovery of Guiana he could have said what Waugh said about his excursion from Georgetown to Brazil and back: "It makes no claim to being a spiritual odyssey." The chaplain could not afford the luxury of a spiritual odyssey in search of a visionary City: there was too much to be done to keep that part of the earthly city to which he was committed from becoming thoroughly disconnected. Besides, he was a merciful realist who knew better in that fungus-nurturing humidity than to give a sermon that lasted more than two minutes. Jones, the mad charismatic who, like Hitler, had the burden of a whole world on his shoulders, could get his congregations up in the middle of the night and ramble on for hours.

Certainly the jungle, whether seen from aloft or at ground level, was a blank check one could fill out in terms of one's dearest apprehensions. Some said there were cannibals in it. Once as Officer of the Day, in fact, I had an encounter with what I at first took to be a cannibal. The Sergeant of the Guard and I were returning by jeep at daybreak after having inspected a radio checkpoint about five miles into the jungle. Suddenly, as we jolted along the twisting cartpath, a bronzed and virtually naked man was in front of us, imperiously holding up his hand. The sergeant braked to a stop, pulling his forty-five out of his holster and laying it on his lap as he did so. The cannibal, looking menacing enough with his bad teeth and tangled hair, asked us politely if we would wait a minute. Twenty yards behind him a fellow cannibal with a handful of bananas was climbing down from a tree. Would we like to have them for a shilling? His well-modulated British English suggested that he might have been schooled and decannibalized by the nuns at Georgetown. I gave him two shillings and we drove on, eating the gorgeous tree-ripened bananas.

To judge from available reports, the category of cannibal is a spacious one. In fact, not all cannibals have been people-eaters. In his *Discoverie of Guiana* Ralegh speaks of a "nation of inhumaine Canibals" who would "for 3 or 4 hatchets sell the sonnes and daughters of their owne brethren and sisters" but he never says that they ate anybody. In Montaigne's well-known essay "Of Cannibals," we learn that the cannibals of Brazil had a society that put civilized Europe to shame. Indeed, it was not far short of the standard set by those denizens of the Golden Age about whom Don Quixote tells the respectful but bored goatherds shortly after his encounter with the brave Biscayan. Montaigne's cannibals—who make an appearance in Shakespeare's *The Tempest,* by way of John Florio's translation, when Gonzalo describes his ideal commonwealth—believed in the immortality of the soul, respected their priests and prophets, were brave in war and affectionate in marriage. They wouldn't have felt too out of place in the Garden of Eden, about which Ralegh writes at great length in his *History of the World.* If they did occasionally eat a captured enemy it was only after they had treated him well and fed him "every sort of delicacy." Clearly, Waugh's Tony Last would have been more comfortable with them than with the Dickens fanatic, James Todd. To them, and no doubt to Montaigne as well, the people of Jonestown would have been barbarians. It is pleasant to think that my banana cannibal might have descended from them.

Georgetown was nobody's idea of the Shining City, but it had its own attractions, few of which Waugh had time to observe in his two short visits. Canals ran down the pleasantly wide streets, originally laid out by the Dutch; St. George's Cathedral was then the second highest wooden building in the world, and the city itself was much admired for its well-preserved and stilted wooden structures; the Georgetown Cricket Club could boast of the finest cricket grounds in the tropics, and when the match was over, spectators could repair to their favorite nightclubs convinced that they would hear the best calypso music in the Caribbean; high tea at the hotel Sunday afternoon (one learned to ignore the weevils that had been baked into the bread) was the prandial event of the week; and there in the "Land of the Six Peoples" it was pleasant to get the same British English from a Black cab driver or an East Indian hotel clerk that one got from the Jesuits at Sunday mass.

In order to compose my mind before the radio program, I sometimes visited the Botanical Gardens, as famous in Guiana as Central Park is in America and a good deal safer to stroll in. Sea cows (manatees) lived in its small lake, and for two shillings I could get a native boy to whistle one up from the bottom. Its bovine head would emerge unbelievably from the muddy water; I could pet its slimy nose while the boy fed it a handful of marsh grass. Ralegh too had seen a sea cow, a great fish "as big as a wine pipe," and learned that it was "most excellent and holsome meate." I was told that on an island in the middle of the lake there were alligators whose habit was to eat the young egrets that hatched there. I saw the egrets but not the alligators. Ralegh, however, had seen "thousands of those vglie serpents" and even saw one devour "a Negro, a very proper young fellow."

Ralegh, who among many other things was a gardener, would have loved the

Botanical Gardens. On his well-farmed estate in Ireland (where he and Edmund Spenser sometimes read their poems to one another) he planted potatoes and yellow wallflowers he had imported from the Azores. During his long second incarceration in the Bloody Tower, he was allowed to keep a garden in which he grew herbs. His lengthy treatment of the Garden of Eden in his *History of the World* is no doubt a reflection of his horticultural bent. He was fascinated with the depiction of Alcinous's garden in Book VII of *The Odyssey* and was convinced that Eden had been Homer's grand model. Surely he would have been delighted with the great hydroponic garden (one of the first in the world) which the U. S. Army had built at Atkinson Field. He would have realized that such an artificially accelerated garden was a controlled exploitation of those cannibal-like forces of the jungle against which the army engineers at Atkinson as well as the pathetic doomsday people in Jonestown had to do endless battle.

For Ralegh, universal man that he was, gardening and pharmacy were hard to separate. In the Tower he made pills, a tonic of strawberries, and a "Great Cordial," also known as his "Balsam of Guiana"—a smorgasbord mixture of ingredients that included spirits of wine, hart's horn, mint, gentian, sugar, and sassafras. This witch's brew was not only recommended by Queen Ann of Austria but was internationally famous. Ralegh had some of it sent to his protégé, the dying Prince Henry, but it arrived too late to save him. Don Quixote too claimed to have a "balsam of Fierabras" so powerful that it could instantly repair a broken body, but since it existed only as a recipe in his head it was of no use to him after he had lost part of his ear in the battle with the Biscayan.

Montaigne's cannibals favored a less mystical concoction—a drink made from roots, claret in color, "not at all heady, but wholesome to the stomach." The drink Tony Last was given by the Pie-wie natives when he and James Todd dropped in on one of their celebrations was so heady that it knocked him out for two days, during which time he missed the visitors who would have been his last chance to return to civilization. Far less potent, though widely acclaimed throughout the Caribbean in my time, was Limacol, a lotion compounded mainly of lime juice and alcohol. When applied to face or head, especially after a hard night, it had a wonderfully bracing effect, and when taken internally, as a friend told me, was a quick but not lasting cure for constipation. But nothing could compare for sheer potency and permanency of effect with that other Balsam of Guiana (strawberry Flavour-aide laced with cyanide and tranquilizers) which the Reverend Jim Jones, that frightful

Man of La Mancha, administered to 918 members of his People's Temple to speed their departure from his Infernal City.

In September I was elevated to Troop Commander, and the radio program had to be abandoned. I missed my weekly trip to Georgetown, perhaps not as much as Ralegh missed Guiana after his first trip, but still I missed it. Before long I was recalled to division headquarters at West Palm Beach where I spent a comfortable winter and saw much of that American Bower of Bliss, Palm Beach, which, unlike Waugh's London, was then recovering grandly from the austerities of the war. Perhaps Ralegh, his experience in the Bloody Tower having tempered the utopian enthusiasms that had marked his Guiana adventure, would have identified Palm Beach as one of those "vicious countries" about which he writes in his *History of the World*: in them "nature being liberal to all without labour, necessity imposing no industry or travel, idleness bringeth no other fruits than vain thoughts and licentious pleasures."

Back in civilian life I repeated Ralegh's experience; having discovered Guiana, my attention had become programmed and I kept rediscovering it, often in the most unlikely places. Political developments caught my eye even when their treatment by the media indicated that the world generally considered them of little moment. Thus I saw British Guiana cease to be a crown colony and, after an interval of civic unrest as the East Indians under Cheddi Jagan contended with the Africans under Forbes Burnham, become the Cooperative Republic of Guyana. Then there were the inevitable major and minor atrocities, aimed as usual at a greater unity, that made small headlines or caught international attention when they took more dramatic form—when, for instance, a Jesuit priest was stabbed to death while photographing an anti-government rally. It was a native of Guyana, Leakh Narayan Bhoge, who, working as a double agent for the FBI, helped to ensnare the Soviet spy, Zakharov. A few years ago, when a Canadian mining company went public with its plans to cooperate with the government of Guyana in the development of its potentially rich gold mines, the Canadian government expressed concern about the country's poor record on human rights.

No doubt the prospect of Guyana gold was as attractive to Cheddi Jagan or Forbes Burnham as in Ralegh's day it had been to Queen Elizabeth of England or Philip II of Spain. The country was as hard up as one might expect a largely managed economy to be. In my day a Guianese dollar (a document as flamboyantly colored as a tropical bird) was worth eighty-five cents American, but I gather from a travel book that now an American dollar will get you from ten to twenty Guyana dollars, depending on where you go shopping for your money. The same book warns against walking out alone at night in Georgetown, whether for fear of cruising Amazons or hungry cannibals it does not say. In my day the worst I had to fear was a not too insistent prostitute or a youngster wanting a stick of gum. I like to imagine that one of those youngsters was Cheddi Jagan himself, the East Indian dentist who later became Prime Minister and was even pictured on the front page of the *New York Times* as he conferred in the White House with President John F. Kennedy. Kennedy would have had reason to be wary of Jagan, who apparently had dreams of building his own Marx-inspired City in which all things would connect. But the picture is especially interesting given the fact that the young president was himself the inspiration for a dream of Camelot that quickly proved to be as much an idol of the mind as Manoa was for Ralegh.

News of Waugh's sudden death on Easter Sunday in 1966 was another sad connection with my Demerara days, but for sheer drama no connections could compete with the mass suicide at Jonestown in November of 1978. The latter was much on my mind the following spring as I pursued Ralegh to the Bloody Tower of London. On Pentecost Sunday I saw where he lived during the thirteen years of his second incarceration and where, with the assistance of many others, including Ben Jonson, he wrote his *History of the World*. There was room for his family and servants, and friends could visit him. He had with him a chest of books and papers; he had easy access to his garden and to a terrace with a view of the Thames where he could take his exercise. He had his numerous projects to keep him busy, including experiments with ways of distilling fresh water from salt water and preserving meat for sea voyages. He dispensed his pills and his Balsam of Guiana and cured his own tobacco. Some believed that he had plenty of time left over to plot and scheme: King James, for instance, suspected he was involved in the Gunpowder Plot. He complained of the cold and damp and suffered from various ailments, but surely there were many at Jonestown who would gladly have changed places with him, and surely there were moments during his second trip to Guiana when he yearned for the relative security and comfort of his Tower apartment.

Nevertheless, like the famous lions that were caged elsewhere in the Tower, his thrusting spirit was in chains. He was out of favor with the king, reprieved but legally guilty and under sentence of death, and the future was dark. In fact, it had looked so dark while he was waiting trial for treason that he attempted suicide. He had to live with the thought that the results of his first voyage had fallen far short of his and others' expectations and that some even refused to believe that he had gone on the voyage—had hidden out in Cornwall because he was "too easeful and sensuall to undertake a jorney of so great travel." There must have been times when he remembered the "digression touching our mortality" in his *History*, in which he had written of the seventh and last age of man that it is a time when "with many sighs, groans, and sad thoughts" we come by a crooked way "to the house of death, whose doors lie open at all hours, and to all persons."

He had to live too with the knowledge that many who did not doubt that he had discovered Guiana had doubts about the veracity of his report. Too much of it sounded like a fairy story: Amazons meeting with men in an annual springtime party in order to conceive and continue their race; men with heads beneath their shoulders; men living in trees and oysters growing in trees; a 110-year-old man who walked twenty-eight miles a day; a City of Gold. A Gresham's law of discovery was working against him: by the end of the sixteenth century there were too many fabulous stories about fabulous places. Evelyn Waugh, returning from Guiana in the blasé twentieth century, had the same experience, if on a reduced scale. He had brought home a crate of stuffed baby alligators as gifts for children, but the recipients were unimpressed. One youngster thought his alligator was a rabbit; a girl named hers "Evelyn" and tore it to pieces.

Montaigne in "Of Cannibals" claims to have gotten his information from "a plain ignorant fellow," who was "therefore more likely to tell the truth" without exaggerating it to make a better story. This, of course, did not keep Montaigne from using the plain fellow's report in order to enhance his own story of the paradoxical superiority of cannibal culture to the culture of Western Europe. Ralegh, of course, was neither plain nor ignorant, but he was looking for a City, and the fabulousness of the objective helped to determine his standard of credibility. Deep in the Guiana jungle, where it was believed that both men and oysters could be found in trees, the story that somewhere in the jungle one man was forced to spend his life reading to another would be as credible as the story of a tribe that had committed suicide at the behest of a charismatic leader. Thus the fabulousness of plain reality conspires against the effort to distinguish between fable and history. My own encounter with the banana cannibal, who loomed up so fabulously before me in the daybreaking jungle, made it easier for me to believe thirty-three years later that the mass suicide at Jonestown had really happened.

When Waugh refused to claim that his own discovery of Guiana had been a spiritual odyssey, he was in effect saying that he was in a position to write the kind of trustworthy history that Montaigne preferred. It meant also that he was biased for St. Augustine's distinction between the City of God and the City of Man and skeptical of all attempts to confuse the two. Ralegh was closer to this position when he wrote his *History* than he had been in the days of his first Guiana odyssey, but to Jim Jones the distinction must always have been meaningless. When, trapped in the fable of his paranoia, he got to the point of claiming that he was the reincarnation of Christ and Lenin, he was trying to build a City that would have invalidated Augustine by transcending history altogether. Here we can see how inevitable was the Soviet claim that the CIA had murdered the people of Jonestown to keep them from emigrating to the USSR: as if the Soviets, those builders of a secular City of God, could honestly imagine no other destination for them.

Nevertheless, there was ample American precedent for Jones's effort. When his lawyer, Charles Garry, called Jonestown "a jewel that the whole world should see," he was echoing, whether he knew it or not, the famous words of Puritan John Winthrop: "For we must consider that we will be as a City upon a Hill. The eyes of all people are upon us..." The ringing words occur in the sermon "A Model of Christian Charity," which Winthrop, the first governor of Massachusetts Bay Colony, preached somewhere in the middle of the Atlantic Ocean as his ship, the *Arabella*, headed for the heroic enterprise of City building in that New World that Ralegh had done so much to publicize.

But there would be trials and tribulations aplenty in the discovery of that New World and the attempt to build a Shining City in it. "The Wilderness through which we are passing to the Promised Land," Cotton Mather would write later, "is all over fill'd with Fiery flying serpents." It was an experience that Ralegh had had more than once in Guiana, perhaps never more memorably than on that day when, boating through "the most beautiful cuntrie that euer mine eies beheld...the Deere came downe feeding by the waters side, as if they had beene vsed to a keepers call." Yet two sentences later in that Edenic setting, the very proper young Negro goes for a swim and is devoured by an alligator.

One may wonder how often later—back in the Bloody Tower then and writing his *History* so that mortality would have been much on his mind—Ralegh remembered that dramatic proof that Paradise was, as Augustine believed, forever denied to the City of Man. Waugh with his Augustinian bias would have been prepared to expect the alligator, and certainly the comic artist in him would have relished the reversal of expectations. Indeed, such a reversal is at the heart of *A Handful of Dust* as Tony Last's search for the secular City of his dreams ends up, contrary to anything Montaigne might have led him to expect, in a secular hell. He was no more prepared for Cotton Mather's fiery flying serpents than the beguiled utopians of Jonestown were. The recognition of this fact is what causes him to say in the delirium of the fever that finally yields to James Todd's jungle medicine: "I will tell you what I have learned in the forest, where time is different. There is no City."

There is reason to believe that if Ralegh had lived to write an account of his second discovery of Guiana he would have expressed the same conclusion. Things had not connected. He had lost his son Wat in the disastrous encounter with the hated Spanish, who all along had represented a threat to his cause, next to whom Amazons, cannibals, and hungry alligators were minor annoyances. "My braynes are broken," he wrote to his loyal and thoroughly admirable wife as he headed for home and the Bloody Tower, expecting the worst. He was taken on a cold October morning to the Old Palace Yard of Westminster to be executed. On the way he was given a cup of sack. One can imagine that under the circumstances he would have preferred some of his own Balsam of Guiana.

Before he served up the lethal cocktail to his congregation, Jim Jones announced that "It is time to die with dignity." Ralegh in any event died with all the dignity one would have expected from a man who was, as the antiquary John Aubrey later wrote, "one of the gallantest worthies that ever England bred." Addressing the assembled multitude from the scaffold, he spoke with moving eloquence for a good half hour, wanting like the dying Hamlet to have his cause reported aright to the unsatisfied, but seeing no Horatio who would do it for him. Among other things he confessed to "being a great sinner of a long time and in many kinds, my whole course a course of vanity, a seafaring man, a soldier and a courtier."

Afterwards he knelt on the gown that the executioner had spread for him and prayed. Then he put his head on the block, but the headsman still hesitated so that Ralegh, hovering on the brink of his last discovery, was forced to cry: "Strike, man, strike!" His head came off at the second blow of the ax.

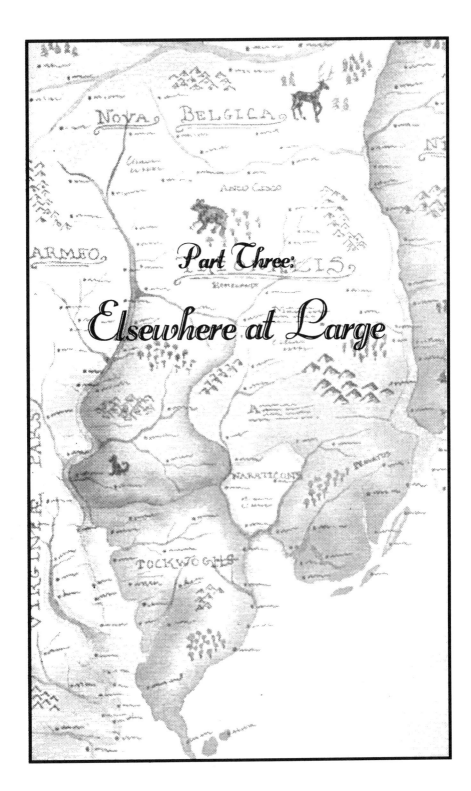

Part Three:

Elsewhere at Large

Correspondences
1979

ome from our Grand Tour and recovered from jet lag, my wife and I saw that in the interval the world continued to deconstruct toward the ultimate entropy, and that morale, especially in the United States, had continued to deteriorate. Everyone agreed with the President that we were experiencing a grave crisis of confidence. In a lecture at Harvard, Patricia Harris, Secretary of Housing and Urban Development, blamed our low morale on the intellectuals' lack of nerve and their failure to find and articulate a national purpose— a failure compounded by the unrealistic insistence that government officials assume the superstar status of movie idols in the '30s and the '40s. In much the same vein, and using the recent death of John Wayne as his springboard, *New York Times* columnist Tom Wicker saw a clear connection between our present lassitude and our inability to distinguish between political realities and Hollywood-nurtured illusions.

We were staying in Bloomsbury—itself the locus of many failed illusions—when John Wayne's death was announced on placards at all newsstands and with front-page headlines in all newspapers. The world was full of news that day to jar our high morale: letter bombs in the north of England, aftershocks of the DC-10 crash at Chicago, violence at the gas pumps in America, civil war in Nicaragua, the agonies of the boat people in the South China Sea, the murder trial of British parliamentarian Jeremy Thorpe, business as usual with the Red Brigades in Italy and the IRA in Northern Ireland, the threat of a strike by the London Underground employees, inflation rampant everywhere. Wayne's death overwhelmed it all.

Wayne died as the traditional hero should: in effect with his boots on, in high morale, fighting his adversary, cancer, to the end. Indeed, there seemed to be almost universal agreement that the image of the traditional hero was the only one appropriate for him. Newsweek referred to his life as a saga. The actress Louise Brooks remembered thinking, when she saw Wayne for the first time, "This is no actor but the hero of all mythology."

There were dissenters, of course—native skeptics for whom the true hero is the uncompromising exposer of all heroics—but on the whole it was as if El Cid had slain his last Saracen and passed on to glory. And as with El Cid, the distinction between historical person and legendary role was not considered relevant.

Who is the true hero? In Carlyle's house in Chelsea I saw a copy of *On Heroes and Hero-Worship* in a bookcase and wondered what Carlyle would have thought of Wayne. To Carlyle, for whom Napoleon was the last great man, the hero is inspired and inspiring, sincere, "a voice direct from Nature's own heart," and therefore in touch with truth. It may not be easy for an age to find the hero it needs to save it from ruin, but when he is found he must be revered with "an obedience that knows no bounds." I have an uneasy feeling that for most readers today Carlyle points more toward Jim Jones and Jonestown than toward John Wayne. Certainly Jones tried something on the grand scale and in the process commanded an obedience that knew no bounds, and Carlyle, I suspect, would have given him some credit for that. Wayne, on the other hand, was a Hollywood creation and thus, by Carlyle's lights, a prisoner of the mere outer shows of existence. Besides, democratic America, "a place sunk deep in cant, twaddle, and hollow traditionality," is not the soil out of which Carlyle expected heroes to grow.

Emerson was often at Carlyle House during his Grand Tour. His own series of lectures on heroes, *Representative Men*, had recently been delivered, so the two had the subject in common. Carlyle recognized Emerson as a spiritual son "in a good degree, but gone into philanthropy and other moonshine." What Carlyle identified as moonshine would, I suspect, have made it possible for Emerson to see something heroic in Wayne; at the same time, the Yankee skepticism that made him wary of Brook Farm would probably have alerted him to the moonshine in Jim Jones. But there is something else in Emerson that helps us understand the appeal of Wayne and all heroes, and that is Emerson's total commitment to "the beautiful and heartwarming doctrine of correspondences." The power of the hero to command reverence and obedience depends on his capacity to embody an image in which the potentially contradictory or threateningly anarchic has been brought into a state of harmonious correspondence. Like the figures in the Dewar's Scotch advertisements, like Emerson himself, the hero has got his head and his act together.

If, as Carlyle says, it is hard for an age to find the hero it needs, Wayne (and Jones as well) had the good fortune to live in an age so wracked with discordances that his fans were practically driven into his arms. Whether he himself saw the discrepancy between the illusion and reality—whether he, in fact, lied to himself—is another matter.

Not that popular images of correspondence are in short supply to the American abroad, who can find everywhere morale-supporting continuities with home. There is disco dancing in Paris, London, and Dublin, and the dancers, at least while they are dancing, seem blessedly beyond all contradiction—indeed, beyond all sense of their troublesome separate selves. McDonald's hamburgers, Colonel Sanders's fried chicken, Coca-Cola and Pepsi-Cola, and American-style jeans do the work that translation does; like the Rosetta Stone, which we saw in the British Museum the day John Wayne died, they close the gap between languages and assert themselves as symbolic forces that will save the times from ruin.

On the Left Bank there are nearly as many places to buy hot dogs as there are art galleries. In Paris and London the young clutch and nuzzle one another with the same unawareness of the discordant world around them as they have in America. In Paris lovers meet clandestinely in the famous Père-Lachaise cemetery, and there in the presence of the glamorous dead move in rapport with ancient celestial harmonies, just as lovers did 500 years ago in the Cemetery of the Innocents. Apart from one another, they leave notes in the crevices of the monument of Frédéric Chopin, with whom, before he became a monument, Emerson had dinner in London. Lovers are even better at conveying a sense that all is well with the world than the omnipresent transcendental meditators, whose appetite for correspondence was fed in Paris by Baba Ram Dass's lecture on TM and allied subjects shortly before we arrived.

Everywhere there are joggers: along the Seine, along the Thames, along the Liffey, in the Bois de Boulogne, in Hyde Park, in Stephen's Green. Every morning a rangy, handsome man, beautifully decked out in blue and white, jogged by our hotel on rue Jacob, turned down rue Bonaparte, and came back on rue Visconti, passing the house where Racine died unheroically, Carlyle believed, simply because Louis XIV had once looked sternly on him. The Irish seem to jog less than the English (it may have something to do with the Reformation), but still they jog. Outside of Kildare (to Carlyle, a wretched, wild village) we saw a young man come over the crest of a jewel-green pasture and lope along gracefully among the grazing sheep—a scene so overwhelming in its pastoral simplicity that it lingered in our imaginations like a harbinger of universal peace.

Joggers are in a state of correspondence and in touch with larger harmonies. There is something of the hero's concentration and dedication in them, something of the discipline of the fundamentalist Christian that makes President Carter the inevitable jogger. Up hill and down dale they go, in fair weather or foul, with the hero's unshakable morale, as if dedicated to keeping not simply themselves but the times from ruin.

But the best of all images of correspondence are the European subways, and especially the wonderful Paris Métro, in which the points of connection that integrate the system are called *correspondances*. The subway systems of Paris and London (perhaps one should add the Paris sewers) model a state of unity-in-complexity that mocks the demoralizing incapacity of human beings to achieve something approaching it on a moral, social, or a political level. In some ways the Métro is better than jogging, better than love, better even than the heroic version of Wayne himself, as a vision of clarity and coherence. Perhaps this is why it can be so unnerving when, as sometimes happens in London, a rush-hour train stops inexplicably between stations. In the almost unbearable dead silence what does one hear if not the whispering of an ultimate chaos that the correspondent system had so effectively muffled?

Emerson in his transcendental fashion would have spun allegories out of all this, as he would have with the pigeon that hopped aboard our car at one of the open-air stops on the Circle Line subway in London. Unconcerned with the passengers who stepped delicately around him, he gobbled up the edible debris on the floor. He was still there gorging himself when we got off at Notting Hill Gate. We imagined him continuing his own Grand Tour: High Street, Kensington, Gloucester Road, South Kensington, Sloan Square, Victoria Station, the Embankment, perhaps hopping off finally at Tower Hill, crop full and in high morale in a new pigeon world. The ideal tourist, he traveled light and lived off the land; the very model of Emersonian self-reliance, he was immediately at home in all social climates.

Unless like the French critic and novelist Alain Robbe-Grillet you believe that all metaphors are lies, the pigeon is one kind of correspondent hero. But so is Charlie the Revlon girl, beaming from the pages of American women's magazines. We met her British cousin in a copy of *Charlie News*, a four-page tabloid someone had left in our compartment on the train from Bath to London. Charlie, according to the banner headline, is LOOKING GOOD—FEELING GREAT. She is svelte, outgoing, vibrantly alive, and like the women in the Virginia Slims ads, has her head and act gloriously together. A few centuries ago Beau Nash would have been happy to have her in his Pump Room at Bath. She is optimistic, enthusiastic, and involved in a range of activities "from makeup to tennis matches to disco fever and everything in between." Her theory about energy, that the best way to get more of it is to spend what you already have, might startle Barry Commoner, but she has apparently proved it out on her own pulse. Marching into the 1980s, she's "got her sights set on her looks and her lifestyle." There are Charlies everywhere from Melbourne to Munich; anointed with Concentrated Eau de Cologne and Concentrated Perfume Spray, glowing with Fresh Eye Color reinforced with the new Soft Smudge for a bit of mystery, they "seem to be the phenomenal wave of the future."

Obviously, the future implied by Charlie would no more inspire the dyspeptic Carlyle than it would Hamlet. "Now get you to my lady's chamber," the latter says with Yorick's skull in his hands, "and tell her, let her paint an inch thick, to this favour she must come." Nevertheless, Charlie, like the image of the correspondent Métro system and the heroic image of John Wayne, helps us keep this bit of bad news in the back corners of our mind. Sid Vicious, like those early seventeenth-century Puritans who in their pious rage smashed holy-water fonts and stained-glass windows at Canterbury, was an anticosmetic force in the world. Indeed, as some *Rolling Stone* readers are willing to believe of him and his fellow Sex Pistols, he was a heroically intransigent attack on bourgeois corruption. Now he keeps company with Yorick's skull. Meanwhile, Charlie is still looking good and feeling great. I thought of her on the flight home as I read "How to Recognize and Enjoy the Real You" by Shirley Conran in the British *Cosmopolitan*. After some bad times, Conran had finally gotten her head and act together and was anxious to pass on this advice from her psychiatrist: "In moments of doubt try repeating to yourself this phrase: 'You're not crazy. They are.' " It's hard to imagine Charlie suffering moments of doubt, but if she ever does, this is the sort of thing she would say.

Still, the news gets through even to the temporarily abstracted tourist: things are bad all over. Perhaps they were never really good. As Voltaire told Boswell on his

Grand Tour, "Nothing is perfect in this damned world." Sufficient for the time is the corruption thereof. Few of us can take comfort from the knowledge that there has always been available a perspective in which the devil is having a field day. As with Watergate or Jonestown, it is always fresh and overwhelming news.

The tourist who had Emerson's habit of seeking out figural correspondences but lacked his optimism could see physical equivalents of moral decay everywhere. The public toilets at the Chartres railroad station are like the doorways to hell. In his notes for *Dubliners* Joyce wrote: "Paris—a lamp for lovers hung in the wood of the world," but it would take Hercules longer to clean the offal and discarded Métro tickets off its streets than it took him to cleanse the Augean stables. The Seine, the Thames, and the Liffey smell bad. In London the whiskey is cut to seventy proof; mendicant rock bands assault your ears in the passageways of the Underground; the station platforms smell of coal smoke, and the approaching train, driving its hollow grinding roar ahead of it through the tunnel, portends an ominous future; drunks fight on the esplanade in front of Westminster Cathedral; the sweating hordes on Oxford Street suggest that the human race in its desperate scramble for subsistence is about to overwhelm itself; teenagers break into Highgate Cemetery, sacred to the memory of Karl Marx, for their midnight orgies. In Dublin someone is always on strike (the Postal Services and McDonald's were the most conspicuous targets while we were there); the heart of the city is unbelievably littered (signs everywhere: "Keep Dublin Tidy"); beggar women with children trained in solicitation accost you boldly (one of them is apprehended with £80 on her person); rampaging teenagers push over headstones in Glasnevin Cemetery, where in Joyce's *Ulysses* Paddy Dignam is buried; and the whiskey is still cut to seventy proof.

Wordsworth, whom Emerson visited on his Grand Tour, believed that Carlyle was sometimes insane and generally "a pest of the English tongue," but agreed with him that the times were sad. "Sin, sin is what he fears," Emerson wrote afterward in his journal. One of the most vigorous passages in *The Prelude* is a description of St. Bartholomew Fair in Smithfield, London, a combination of bazaar, country fair, and freak show—a spectacle of discord that lays "the whole creative powers of man asleep." How would Wordsworth have reacted to the Clignancourt flea market in Paris or the Portobello Road flea market in London—or for that matter to the getting-and-spending hordes on the Champs Elysées, Oxford Street, or O'Connell Street? What is each of these if not an image of "blank confusion! true epitome/Of what the mighty City is herself" if one is predisposed, as so many romantics and Americans are, to measure the world against expectations of pastoral simplicity?

Charlie would fare badly in such a Wordsworthian perspective. Being a lady of bright surfaces and boundless self-generating energy, she is at home in the city—as was Dr. Johnson, if for somewhat different reasons. The Portobello flea market would no more demoralize her than the Champs Elysées, both of which would be moving her phenomenal wave of the future. But Wayne, connected as he is with the pastoral of the American West and the legend of the cowboy, would be on Wordsworth's side. The city is bad news for the cowboy hero: it fences in his spirit and demoralizes him. He prefers the open range for the same reason that Emerson preferred Concord to Boston: in the clutter and the bustle of the bourgeois metropolis he loses his correspondences. Our attraction to him is an expression of that ambivalence about the city on which the legend of John Wayne feeds.

And so to the Martello Tower at Sandycove, where James Joyce lived in 1904 with Oliver St. John Gogarty and Samuel Trench. This was the edifice that was in time to figure in the first chapter of Ulysses, and that is now as sacred a place for literary intellectuals as Marx's monument in Highgate Cemetery is for socialist intellectuals. Joyce's tower connects with Carlyle's last hero, having been built by the British in 1803 as part of defense measures against a threatened Napoleonic invasion; it is therefore a proper place to speculate about heroes. We went there the day after Bloomsday, June 16, which we had celebrated by once again seeing the film *Ulysses*. We stood on the parapet at the point where, we imagined, Buck Mulligan, in the most appropriate possible beginning for a modernist masterwork, parodies the beginning of the Catholic mass as he prepares to shave.

According to Joyce's authorized biographer, Herbert Gorman, the spirit of Ireland "rose like a stone wall between Joyce and the esthetic freedom he demanded, . . . seeking to stifle his independent will, striving to force him into a conformity that was an abnegation of himself, endeavoring to net his soaring impulses with the traditions of years and the authority of the masses." From this "slave civilization" he found his freedom in flight "into the spiritual domain whose air he had to breathe if he was to live. . . . He did not want to live for Ireland (as Ireland was); he wanted Ireland to live for him (as its mythic substance was pictured in his mind)."

Gorman's worshipful solemnities (exactly the sort of overblown language that Joyce effectively parodies in Ulysses) not only reminds one of Shirley Conran's discovery and enjoyment of the Real You, but helps one see, forty years after its publication, that there is a clear line of development from modernism to the human-potential movement. Gorman could have written a biography of Baba Ram Dass or Charlie without shifting gears.

But Gorman helps one see, too, the connection between Joyce and John Wayne. Both represent an elite of chosen light-bearers versus the minions of the force of darkness. For both, it is always a shoot-out at high noon with no quarter given or expected. This is why in their sublime egotism (which they share with Charlie) they can assume that what is good for them is good for culture.

Would Emerson have placed Joyce alongside Goethe as the writer-hero? "Belief consists in accepting the affirmations of the soul; unbelief, in denying them," he writes in *Representative Men*, as if looking ahead to *A Portrait of the Artist as a Young Man*. Certainly he would have recognized that Joyce was like all great writers in that he draws "his rents from rage and pain," that by "acting rashly, he buys the power of talking wisely," that his "first act, which was to be an experiment, becomes a sacrament," and that in his work "the past and present ages, and their religions, politics and modes of thinking, are dissolved into archetypes and ideas."

And what of Carlyle, who expected as little from the Irish as from democratic America? Would he have ranked Joyce along with Samuel Johnson and Robert Burns among the Priesthood of the Writers of Books? Most likely he would have noted that Joyce, unlike Johnson, had not put out of his heart "pride, vanity, ill-conditioned egotism of all sorts," so that he belonged with those writers who are themselves "the summary of all other disorganizations." He would probably have seen in Joyce, as in modernism generally, a repetition of that eighteenth-century skepticism that was unremittingly hostile to all gods and heroes ("Heroes have gone out; Quacks have come in"). Emerson would have agreed with him here. True, in his lecture on Montaigne he had good things to say about skepticism, but he was talking about a creative skepticism that, though it opens abyss under abyss and displaces opinion by opinion, is still grounded on transcendental certainties and has no doubt of an Eternal Cause. Positive skepticism is compatible with writing bibles "to unite again the heavens and the earthly world." It is not likely that Emerson would have seen such a spirit of concordance at work in Joyce.

With skepticism in mind, one is inclined to look eastward from the Martello Tower across the wild Irish Sea to Highgate Cemetery and Karl Marx, a man who had close affinities with the modernists. His heroic features on top of the huge monument suggest that he could have co-starred with John Wayne at any time. "Workers of all lands unite" is lettered across the top of the monument, expressing as an imperative the ancient dream of a final correspondence. Below the memorial plaque there is this famous quotation: "The philosophers have only interpreted the world in various ways. The point however is to change it."

According to Gorman, Joyce got no further into *Das Kapital* than the first sentence, which he thought absurd. Perhaps he made this point to Lenin if, as has been suggested, the two actually did meet in a Zurich café not long before the latter traveled in his sealed train to the Finland Station. Still, both Joyce and Marx aspired to an order beyond interpretation, beyond mere point of view and ideology, beyond politics and history and out of time. In Marx's grand vision the state would have withered away and political science would be over; similarly, with *Ulysses* Joyce attempted, as the critic Eugene Goodheart puts it, "to realize Mallarmé's ambition to put the whole world between the covers of a book and make subsequent literature unnecessary, by exhausting all the possibilities of representation and expression." The effort to achieve this degree of finality, in which all competing voices and perspectives are excluded, is, as we know, a characteristic of totalitarianism. And there is indeed a kind of totalitarianism in modernism. Hitler and Jim Jones wished to create societies as self-contained and resistant to hostile and demoralizing points of view as the masterworks of Joyce, Pound, and Proust.

Totalitarianism, whether aesthetic or social, is utterly hostile to established religions, which ask the individual to acknowledge perspectives and realties that transcend art and the dialectical operations of the material world. For Marx, "the abolition of religion, as the illusory happiness of men, is a demand for their real happiness." Joyce abjures Catholicism, even at the cost of refusing to give comfort to his dying mother, not because there is no way of reconciling the aesthetic and religious impulses, but because the artist, as Joyce conceives him, the modernist way, is himself a priest in a counter-religion. Just as Marxism depends on a bourgeois middle class that will stand fast and play its assigned role in the dialectic drama, so the modernist artist needs not a religion that will adapt itself to his needs but one that will stand fast so that he can forge himself against it.

In the *Communist Manifesto* Marx, observing the inevitable consequences of capitalism in society, writes: "All that is solid melts into air, all that is holy is profaned. . . ." In the transgressive, demystifying, revisionary, and desacralizing atmosphere of modernism there is even less room for the hero than there was in Carlyle's skeptical eighteenth century. The modernist skeptic makes room only for the artist hero, who is known by his capacity to reveal the fraudulence of all other pretenders to heroism—and sometimes even, as modernism gives way to postmodernism, to reveal his own fraudulence.

Or put it this way: all true revisions are expected to be downward. Indeed, one perennial theme of the Grand Tour is the discovery of illusion. Boswell on his way home, for instance, had not only learned to scale down his naive estimation of Rousseau but even managed, between Paris and Dover, to make love thirteen times to the latter's mistress, Thérèse Le Vasseur. Meanwhile, Charlie the Revlon girl falls victim to the same revisionary spirit in such exposé novels about the cosmetic industry as Peter Engel's *High Gloss* and Anne Maybury's *Radiance*, which promise to probe beneath the fraudulently alluring facade of beautiful faces and elegant possessions to reveal beauty's backside. The compulsion that melts Charlie into air can melt not only John Wayne but Joyce and Marx as well. Then, unless we have managed to achieve the cool autonomy of the Circle Line pigeon, or at least the narcissistic self-assurance of Shirley Conran, there may be nothing left for us in a world of cosmetic fictions but jogging.

Such dire possibilities were apparently very much on Patricia Harris's mind at Harvard when she traced our low morale to the failure of the intellectuals to find and articulate a national purpose. But the problem for intellectuals is that the deracinating ethos of the Martello Tower has possessed the intellectuals so long now that their inclination is to look with suspicion on any enterprise that promises to raise morale. True, since the Enlightenment, it has always been possible to bewitch some intellectuals with utopian visions of an absolutely correspondent society, but the bewitchment has generally resulted in disconcerting oversimplifications of political realities. Joyce apparently looked on World War II as a conspiracy to keep people from reading *Finnegans Wake*. Such a mystification of literature cannot survive the demystifications of modernism; and ironically, it is usually the artist himself who is most horrified to discover that he has committed himself to a god that has failed.

The patterns and symbols of the intellectuals' radical folk mythology have not only been passed on to those whose outlook is shaped by intellectuals but have been co-opted quite profitably by the bourgeois order they were initially designed to oppose. The conventions of modernism—particularly the degradation of established pieties and the Joycean conviction that all human institutions are conspiracies against the integrity of the individual—long ago became our identifying social knee

jerks, so that the Martello Tower is now a better metaphor of Babel than of liberation.

Such an environment is not one in which heroes are nurtured. What is
nurtured is the habit of skeptical scrutiny that makes it unlikely that the necessary
heroes will appear, or will be distinguishable from frauds and menaces when they
do appear. No doubt John Wayne was able to get his Congressional medal and Jim
Jones was able to lure his followers into their hellish utopia in part because a lot of
people were tired of not having someone around who at least looked like a hero.
But such success as they had was even more the consequence of the absence of real
heroes to measure them against. From the Martello Tower all heroes are equal and
therefore all dangerous. The elevation encourages a perspective in which it is hard to
tell John Wayne from Sid Vicious, or from that Serbian hijacker who, keeping his
own high-noon appointment, insisted on being flown to Shannon and thereby so
fouled up the Aer Lingus schedules that we were four hours late getting into
Chicago. At such moments one is inclined to agree with the playwright Robert Bolt
that what the age needs is not the boat-rocking, epoch-making hero "but a full crew
of moderate men."

Grim thoughts in a grim world. Nevertheless, it was westward-ho from O'Hare
in high morale on the last leg of our Grand tour: the Black Hills, the Badlands, the
Rockies, Yellowstone Park, the Grand Tetons, the Craters of the Moon, Hell's
Canyon—the fabulous playgrounds of the correspondent Western hero. Our pilot, a
New World man brimming with Emersonian optimism and clearly no more
bothered by Carlyle's skepticism than by the graffiti on beauty's backside, chattered
like a tour guide and tipped us to port and starboard so that everyone could see
everything, as if he could not tolerate the idea that any one of his charges should fail
to experience his own joy in the wonderful country. I remembered John Wayne
again as we soared over the austere and tortuous Snake River canyons, where once I
had been a real cowboy. I thought kindly of him then, and kindly of Charlie and
the Kildare jogger and Baba Ram Dass and Boswell and Emerson and Carlyle and
Karl Marx. Peace to them all, and peace to that contrary and troubled man, James
Joyce, who, it always pleased his wife to think, was buried so close to the Zurich Zoo
that he could hear the lions roar.

The Worm in the Big Apple
1981

n Europe my wife and I were always aware that we were moving about in a violent world where kidnappings, purse snatchings, knee-cappings, bombings, and assassinations were as common as soccer matches, but it was always a media-based awareness; none of it touched us personally. With no sense of menace we walked the day and night streets of Rome, Florence, Venice, Paris, London, and Dublin. When an Oregon dentist we met in the Vatican post office warned us about the perils of the Eternal City (the attempted assassination of the Pope having happened within the week) we thought he was a bit paranoid.

Thus it was without apprehension that we began to plan for a trip to New York. We supposed that it had its share of the violence that everyone knows is endemic to American cities, but like the currency, it would be something we were familiar with. I even thought of booking quarters in the Piccadilly Hotel on 45th Street, where in the heart of the theater district I had spent happy times during World War II. Then New York seemed a haven from all that was unpleasant or menacing: an enclave of delight from which one returned to the grimmer, bloodier, or more boring business from which one had been all too briefly furloughed. After my last visit I lived for a while in the jungles of British Guiana (now Guyana). The conviction that I would in due time return to my haven on 45th Street helped to sustain me in a place in which only a madman like the late Reverend Jim Jones could see utopian possibilities.

As we began our homework it quickly became clear that 45th Street was out. A special February issue of *New York* magazine devoted to protecting oneself against crime announced that "it's time for New Yorkers to deal with the reality of life on our precarious streets," and went on to detail the menaces that lay in wait for us on the street, in the subways, in Central Park, in the parking lot, in the lobby, in the elevator, in the apartment. Nicholas Pileggi's article, "Meet the Muggers," in a subsequent issue increased our uneasiness. We learned from Adam Smith in *Esquire* that New York had 1,814 murders in 1980, three times as many as all of Canada, and ten times as many as Tokyo, and that the white-collar class had become a flock of pigeons to the more violent members of what Ken Auletta was calling the underclass. Apparently there was a worm in the Big Apple. We wondered if it wouldn't be wiser to go back to Europe and the more familiar threats of the IRA, the Red Brigades, and the motor-scooter purse snatchers.

In the end, however, we went to New York and, as a result of a shared taxi ride from LaGuardia airport, passed by the Dakota where the late John Lennon had lived and violently died. It looked as peaceful as the neighborhood of our own apartment. Down on 55th Street, five floors below us, women of all ages walked confidently alone even after dark, apparently never having read Nicholas Pileggi or Adam Smith. Sometimes in the middle of the night a horse cab would go clip-clopping along the empty street, as if the cabbie were taking his fares (lovers, no doubt) through a time warp where clocks and death had no dominion.

Nevertheless, the world around us remained violent, as everyone agreed. Central America was in turmoil; Great Britain and Argentina were battling over the Falklands; the Israelis were going after the PLO in Lebanon; Ayatollah Khomeini was vigorously pursuing his holy war with Iraq; terrible things continued to happen to Solidarity in Poland; the soccer world was anticipating that the World Cup matches would be, as usual, a continuation of war by other means; Jonathan Schell's *The Fate of the Earth* was telling us once more that our lives ride on a nuclear hair-trigger; and over in New Jersey taxicab drivers were trying to get permission to carry guns.

Whatever violence is, most people appeared to assume, like Tolstoy and Gandhi, that we would be better off if we had less of it and best off if we had none of it, as if it were evil itself. This bias was being given support by the National Institute of Mental Health, which had just released a much-commented-on ninety-four page report claiming scientific evidence for a cause-and-effect connection between TV violence and violence in the playground and on the street. *Newsweek* was wondering whether we might not be breeding a nation of mild paranoiacs. In the *New York Times* Tony Schwartz, blaming the violence on the priority the networks place on commercial success, conceded that "violence has a place in drama, but unnecessary violence does not." Unnecessary violence included "gratuitous" violence, "designed to arouse a reaction, rather than advance a story legitimately" and excessive in that its level is "out of proportion to ordinary experience."

It is this excessiveness, this lack of apparent proportionality, that leads us to speak of meaningless violence. Adam Smith, who gives two frightening examples of such excessive violence in Manhattan (murders that had nothing to do with the success of the robberies), quotes Charles Silberman's *Criminal Violence, Criminal Justice*: the new thing is that people "kill, maim, and injure without reason or remorse." For many people the murder of John Lennon is more disturbing than killings by the IRA or the Red Brigades: the latter announce reasons we can understand even if we cannot sympathize with their causes. What is more natural, more human, than to kill those who stand between you and ideal justice? Indeed, one of the great attractions of psychiatry is its promise to translate apparently meaningless violence into everyday daylight terms and thus humanize it—even to enrich the translation with optional meanings, as the trial of John Hinckley was then demonstrating. This means, of course, that few psychiatrists would agree with Silberman's statement. Adam Smith gives as an example of a senseless murder a mugger's killing of a young attorney because "I don't like your face." If we gave the mugger the psychiatric in-depth reading we have learned to give poems and novels, his stated reason for the killing might appear both understandable and proportionate; we might even learn to give him that measure of sympathy we give the violent killers in Truman Capote's *In Cold Blood*, the Bonanno family in Gay Talese's *Honor Thy Father*, or Steve Rojack in Norman Mailer's *An American Dream*.

One night, after returning scatheless from a walk through the lower regions of Central Park, we watched a TV interview with Arnold Schwarzenegger, the former Mr. Universe and now the star of *Conan the Barbarian*, the subject of a tumultuous preview at the Rivoli theater some weeks before we arrived on the scene. He seemed a pleasant and physically impressive young man, just the sort of companion with whom one might go safely anywhere in Central Park. His Conan is a very violent person in a very violent movie. "The narrative is so lumpy," *New York* magazine said, "that only the violence will keep the audience involved." Arnold himself, however, clearly believed that the violence in the movie was neither excessive nor meaningless. In *Conan* blood spurts and detached heads fly as the hero encounters very wicked adversaries who stand between him and the vengeance he seeks for a monstrous wrong. Certainly he proves out the movie's Nietzschean epigraph—that which does not destroy us makes us strong; perhaps more important to quote David Anthony Kraft in the Marvel comic-book treatment of the movie, he "informs us about ourselves, including our darker nature." Given the extent to which we now insist that authentic fiction and drama give us information about our lower nature (our higher nature being hopelessly compromised by hypocrisies and verbal fictions), that puts *Conan* in some pretty fast company.

It also puts the movie in the company of fairy stories, and Kraft might have quoted Bruno Bettelheim's *The Uses of Enchantment* in defense of his contention that the violence in *Conan* serves a serious and even didactic purpose. Certainly, like the fairy stories about which Bettelheim writes so perceptively, it connects with our common fantasy-heritage by way of a story that puts justice before charity as it uses violence for purposes of hyperbolical clarification. Modeling virtues familiar to readers of epic literature (to say nothing of soccer fans), it teaches how to cope in extremely adversative circumstances. Conan, in fact, is in complete agreement with Jonathan Schell's much-quoted remark: "Two paths lie before us. One leads to death, the other to life"—which may indicate that there is a powerful element of heroic fantasy in Schell's book. It is quite possible that *Conan* caters less to our appetite for violence than to our appetite for situations in which either/or solutions are indisputably necessary—as they are in the new space game, Star Strike, in which in the comfort of your living room you must "destroy the enemy planet, before it destroys the earth." Conan, in fact, gives comfort not only by depicting but predicting melodrama—that is, the continuation of a world that is neither boring nor overcomplicated. Of course, either/or formulations depend on an extreme censoring of information (necessary for the child, Bettelheim points out) that makes violent consequences likely. This may be why some readers find it hard to reconcile Schell's book with his hopes for a peaceful world.

On the wall of the lobby in the Museum of Natural History we saw a quotation from Theodore Roosevelt that begins: "I want to see you game boys, I want to see you brave and manly" and ends, "Character in the long run is the decisive factor in the life of an individual and of nations alike." Roosevelt, who believed with Shakespeare's good Duke in *As You Like It* that "sweet are the uses of adversity," would have understood and appreciated Conan, and perhaps Star Strike as well.

Conan would have been good to have around for the violent business of San Juan Hill, and surely would have agreed with Roosevelt that the nearly disastrous escapade was a "bully fight" and "great fun." Conan has character, the organization of personality that makes possible the concentration of available powers for significant and, if necessary, violent action. He measures up well against Roosevelt's standard of self-reliance. Like the young mugger whom Adam Smith quotes (and who too might have been useful at San Juan Hill), he likes to support himself.

Meanwhile, the *Village Voice* was reporting on the self-supporting activities of those two ex-jailbirds, Timothy Leary and G. Gordon Liddy, who had recently brought their cross-country debate to New York University and the Beacon theater on the Upper West Side. To many in his audience, Liddy was a classic example of the extent to which character formation can concentrate power for not only violent but anti-individualist purposes. Apparently, four and a half years in prison had strengthened his spirit just as Conan's many brutal years on the mill wheel in the land of the Vanir had strengthened his. Like Schell, he was a "two-paths" man. He too would have been useful at San Juan Hill, where strength of character combined with a capacity for hugger-mugger would have been especially useful. When he told the Beacon theater audience that we "don't give the police enough freedom," Leary called him a Neanderthal—oddly enough, since in Leary's perspective the Neanderthal, not yet having been ruined in the prison of civilization, deserved a less pejorative context.

Leary himself may have more character than he is generally given credit for (after all, he has survived the experience of thirty-nine jails on four continents) but he had little good to say for it. In the Leary lexicon, character is associated with the Protestant ethic and the second law of thermodynamics (the law of entropy) which combine to put in shackles the perfect brain of the child, who is then capable of doing society's violent dirty work with the best will in the world. To him traditional character structure is a Mafia, as is an army, a police force, or a government, and if you wish to learn the extent to which the power concentrated in such human systems is actually a form of pernicious violence, all you have to do is oppose them. Like Tolstoy, he believes that laws make the criminal. Leary would have been no good at all at San Juan Hill; indeed, he would be about as compatible with Roosevelt as he actually was with Eldridge Cleaver when those two met in North Africa some years ago and discovered that they had little more in common than the fact that they were both fugitives.

Of course, when Leary takes his stand in a materialistically tantalizing world against what he conceives the Protestant ethic to be (a means of delaying pleasure), he moves close to some very violent people. In Pileggi's account of street crime in New York, for instance, a detective says of young muggers: "They must be satisfied immediately or they can get very mean. The things they see on television they can never earn enough to buy, and they must go out and get the money any way they can." Such people are as little impressed as Leary is by the Protestant ethic and the law of entropy, and just as likely to define all authority structures as Mafias. Certainly they would endorse the statement he made to his Beacon audience in defense of his use of drugs: "I refuse to permit any government to tell me how to arrange my moods." Of course, Leary could counter (and no doubt has many times) that when the Mafia authorities oppose his quite reasonable and even highly moral preferences they are simply displaying the invalidating violence with which such authorities sustain themselves—and if his words or conduct happen to give comfort to counter-Mafias, the consequences, if any, are ultimately their fault, not his.

One morning we visited the Morgan Library, the memorial of a man who for Leary surely belongs in the Mafia class. There, beside a picture of the great financier, is a portrait of John Milton at age ten, a pretty young man who in time would write an epic sufficiently filled with meaningful violence to satisfy Conan's ardent admirers. The problem is how to interpret it. Looked at one way, the author of *Paradise Lost* is a law-and-order man who favors Leary's detested Mafias. Looked at another way, it is possible to say what Blake says in *The Marriage of Heaven and Hell*: "The reason Milton wrote in fetters when he wrote of Angels and God, and at liberty when of Devils and Hell, is because he was of the devil's party without knowing it." What better and more paradoxical line to take in defense of the individual against the violent lusts of established Mafias? Leary, the cosmic and psychedelic utopian, believing that "We can go as far as we want to," might find in Blake a Milton he can build a future on.

Blake, to whom paradox was as strategically important as it was to Rousseau, also said: "Without contraries is no progression"—a good remark to have in mind when, as we did one beautiful morning, the tourist views the statue (the gift of the Union of Soviet Socialist Republics) on the grounds outside the United Nations buildings. Here a nearly nude green giant is frozen in the act of beating on a huge and already buckled sword. These words are on the pedestal: "We will beat our swords into plowshares." The well-muscled and violently engaged figure suggests

Conan even if his action does not. Conan, we are told at the end of the movie, in time became a king by his own hand, and in that hand, we may be sure, was his trusty and still intact sword. But Conan was not a utopian, and what the statue dramatizes is the utopianism at the heart of Marxism (and at the heart of so much of our thinking about violence as well). Shelley, in whose poetry violent means are so often the necessary preliminary to permanent idyllic and loving conclusions (see, for instance, *Hellas* and *Prometheus Unbound*), probably would have approved of it.

It was good to look at the Soviet statue with Vladimir Bukovsky's essay in the May *Commentary*, "The Peace Movement and the Soviet Union," in mind. Bukovsky spent twelve years in Soviet prisons; most likely the green giant would have suggested to him the paradox of the Soviet direction of the 1980 World Peace Council in Sofia, where, said *Izvestia* in one of its Shelleyesque moods, "The first bright colors have already touched the emerald green parks" and the "golden leaves of maples and aspens are trembling in the breeze." Bukovsky also quotes Lenin's formula for peace—"As an ultimate objective peace simply means Communist world control"—and reminds us that "while comrade Chicherin, at the conference of Genoa in 1922, was appealing to the entire world for total and immediate disarmament, crowds of bewildered people in the Soviet Union were marching to a song that began: 'We'll fan the worldwide flame,/Churches and prisons we'll raze to the ground.'" Bukovsky might prompt one to think that the green giant, being a practical pacifist, is beating not on his own sword but on that of his adversary, where all evil is located.

The Soviet statue was also a good place to contemplate the paradoxical toleration of violence by some of the major pacifist organizations, particularly as the toleration was being presented in the June *American Spectator* by Rael Jean Isaac and Erich Isaac. The Isaacs are impressed with the gap between pacifist rhetoric and reality in the attitude toward the PLO of the American Friends Service Committee, the Fellowship of Reconciliation, and the War Resisters League. They remind us that in 1975 the World Peace Council gave the medal for peace to Yasir Arafat, and that War Resister League President Norma Becker is in favor of overturning all our institutions "because unless these institutions are eradicated it doesn't seem likely that we will be in a position to really practice non-violence." The anarchist Bakunin seems to be implied here, and Leary as well, to say nothing of those members of the Red Brigades recently tried in Rome for having demonstrated the economy of "proletarian justice" by their murder of Aldo Moro: get rid of all establishment

Mafias and the world's great age will begin anew.

Bertrand Russell, who once believed that "the government of New York City was virtually a satellite of the Vatican" and who too had been a jailbird, might have found the Red Brigades a bit uncouth, but he could propose equally extreme solutions: advocating, for instance, that while the United States still had a monopoly on atomic weapons it should use them as a threat to secure worldwide disarmament. He also was a practical pacifist. Like all of his kind he might have been useful at San Juan Hill once he was persuaded that after the conquest there would be no more hills to storm up.

The Isaacs were good at helping us see the semantics of this paradox. They refer to A. J. Muste's radical conception of pacifism in his 1928 essay "Pacifism and Class War," in which he argues that since ninety percent of the world's violence is what maintains the status quo, it is "ludicrous" to urge "rebels against repression" to use nonviolent means. This way out of what is otherwise a dilemma involves not only a distinction between the honorific and pejorative senses in which the term "violence" is used, but a tendency not to use it at all when energy or force in whatever magnitude is being used for approved purposes. Members of the U.S. Peace Council are not likely to see the logo on their official literature (a dove shaped into a clenched fist) as a symbol of violence. For true believers, the Soviet green giant is not depicted in a violent act; he is exerting his considerable virtuous energies against violence. "Violence" has become a dirty word, and to judge from the full-page ad we saw in the *New York Times* for the June 12 National Mobilization for Survival in Central Park ("Abolish Nuclear Weapons Now"), its adequate synonym for a vast number of people is nuclear energy, which in the context of the ad translates as nuclear violence.

Bukovsky calls our attention to an analogous distinction between just and unjust war. Just wars are those fought "in the interest of the proletariat" and "are absolutely justifiable because they lead to the creation of a world in which there will be no more wars, forevermore." No wonder that Marxism-Leninism has always been suspected of being a secularized version of biblical fundamentalism. A just war is like that terminal conflict expected by apocalyptic Christians, after which, as William Martin was pointing out in the June 1982 *Atlantic*, the faithful redeemed will enjoy a new heaven and a new earth. Thus will the *caporegima* of all Mafias, Satan, finally be disposed of. Unfortunately, such a scenario, when read against the history of Western civilization since the Enlightenment, can only remind one of all those

Mafias of virtue militant that, with a noble ruthlessness aimed at a heaven on earth, would make heaven itself seem jejune.

Conan the Barbarian, however, is not only pre-Enlightenment but pre-civilization, and in his movie, as is generally the case in the literature and drama of barbarism, civilization gets a bad press. Such rudimentary civilization as we see, which the audience is no doubt expected to take as an adequate symbol of the civilization it knows, is represented as an effete, demoralized, power-corrupted, and imprisoning place—as easily victimized by a Thulsa Doom as the ramshackle Left was by the Reverend Jim Jones. Conan's world view, like that of Star Strike, is not cluttered up with the ambiguities and paradoxes of power, which is a great source of its attractiveness. His morale is high because he can with singleness of mind use the power available to him. Therefore he is free, whereas civilized man is fettered and easily persuaded to agree with Rousseau in his *Second Discourse*: "When I see multitudes of entirely naked savages scorn European voluptuousness and endure hunger, fire, the sword, and death to preserve only their independence, I feel that it does not behoove slaves to reason about freedom."

Rousseau's ideas about savage life may sound now as if he had early access to and never recovered from Edgar Rice Burroughs, but they have proven influential over the years, in great part because the paradoxical discontents of civilization can still be interpreted as he interpreted them. Utopia is a dream of discontented civilization. Unfortunately, every attempt to realize it has been frustrated because of the very ambiguities and paradoxes of power responsible for the discontents. Hence, no doubt, the appeal of the great pseudo-utopian resource, our darker nature, where power, whether or not defined as violence, can be experienced and enjoyed with an undivided mind.

This, we suspected, was the way it was being experienced in that private fantasy lounge on 54th Street (Live Adult Entertainment—25 Dancers-Hostesses—Free Adult Movies), an ad for which was thrust into our hands every time we came by the corner of Sixth Avenue and 55th Street. And then there was the other fantasy world we walked gingerly through one Sunday afternoon: my old neighborhood around Times Square, where perhaps it was still possible for true believers to imagine that the Protestant ethic and the law of entropy had been canceled, whether or not to Leary's satisfaction, and still possible to accept the Marquis de Sade's paradox that the violence of pornography was the one true way to overcome established Mafias and arrive at utopia. Sade, like Lenin, had a program for a peaceful universe in which the violence of Star Strike would be so patently meaningless that not even children would play it (which may be why French intellectuals with a paradoxical turn of mind, like Michel Foucault, have tended to treat him so respectfully). Perhaps too in a dull time for orgasmic liberationists, Sade could take some comfort from the fact that at the Edison theater up on 47th Street *Oh! Calcutta!*, that *Abie's Irish Rose* of the skin trade, was after these many years still celebrating an erotic black mass once every weekday and twice on Sunday.

There was a time when Bertrand Russell saw some possibilities in Lenin's program, but that time was past when he came to write about Orwell after the latter's death. On that occasion he distinguished himself and Orwell from people like H. G. Wells who did not know that "sensible people have no power." When, following the repeated failure of utopian expectations, this conviction is reinforced by the conviction that all power corrupts (not "tends" to corrupt, as Lord Acton wrote), demoralization and despair are the routine consequences. Too many people then begin to suspect that to insist that the good society be without violence is to insist that it be without power and in love with entropy. "All weakness tends to corrupt," Edgar Z. Friedenberg once wrote, "and impotence corrupts absolutely." If he is right, it is easy to suspect that Jonathan Schell's "sensible" book is on the side of entropy (which, according to Leary's utopian physics, is a thing of the past). Conan, at any rate, acts as if he agrees with Friedenberg.

Occasionally, as we wandered about our apparently peaceful neighborhood, we passed a video-games arcade on Broadway. How sensible were those young people, I wondered, as in fantasy they manipulated great power in violent games? Perhaps the attraction of the arcade was that it was a Conan-like fairy-story world where power could be exercised with great clarity of purpose and high morale: in a place of enchantment locked away from the paradoxes and ambiguities of discontented civilization where it was possible to prove out on one's pulses the truth of Blake's words: "Energy is Eternal Delight." If boredom is the bedfellow of entropy, the video warriors were in an anti-entropic "two paths" enclave, as delighted as Teddy Roosevelt was at San Juan Hill. Perhaps such a place should be read, Bettelheim-fashion, as an anthology of animated fairy stories in which adolescents are taught a lesson without which adult life would be utterly demoralizing: that no matter how technologically sophisticated the world becomes we will continue to be preoccupied with the age-old themes and adversative circumstances, so that, as in *Star Trek*, it will continue to be possible for sensible people to use power wisely. No doubt, many of the warriors, having become expert at fighting off invaders from outer space, would later show up at the Central Park Mobilization to fight for peace.

A little farther south on Broadway, where in the Winter Garden Shakespeare's *Othello* was teaching more disturbing lessons, it was possible to see James Earl Jones, who had fared so badly as Thulsa Doom in *Conan*, be a loser again as the bedeviled Moor. Iago is not of course Bertrand Russell's sensible man as he wields his great power to violent ends; indeed, to us he might seem the epitome of a demoralizing malignity at the very heart of things—as if, analogously, he were technology run wild. So we are tempted, as readers and audiences have always been, to see Othello as an Everyman-loser hopelessly outmaneuvered in the power-corrupted world.

But the play will not let us off that easily, especially when an actor as powerful as Christopher Plummer plays Iago. Othello is not only, as Iago says, "egregiously an ass," but he is woefully ignorant of the darkness within himself, that lower nature about which our culture was in time to entertain such utopian and ultimately disillusioning expectations. He is much more tragically an ass when he insists that Desdemona define herself clearly as "one entire and perfect chrysolite" or as a whore, as if they both belonged in the world of the Soviet green giant, or with Conan the Barbarian in the Hyborian Age.

But what is *Othello* now if not what it has always been: a harrowing dramatic statement about the violent consequences of trying to resolve a complex human situation so absolutely and in such unshaded terms that time will not undo the solution? It is the right play for a time bedeviled with an overload of information and uncertain about the identity of its Iagos. Yet harrowing as it is, there may be some comfort in it for those lovers of New York who are unhappy with the reputation of their beautiful city as an especially violent place. To them the play says that the worm in the Big Apple may simply be the worm in the world.

All for Love: Europe in the Springtime 1981

Love dopes the Western world.
If love be not in the house there is nothing.

Ezra Pound

he great days of the Shakespeare and Company bookstore, when it was located at 12 rue de l'Odeon on the Paris Left Bank, may be behind it, but in its present location across the Seine from Notre Dame Cathedral it is still a place where one can browse in an atmosphere that connotes a legendary past. Here in early June we could buy the *New York Review of Books* and the *Village Voice*. The latter featured a piece by John Berger on Modigliani, then the subject of the exhibition we had recently seen at the Museum of Modern Art in Paris. "The paintings are so widely acknowledged," Berger wrote, "because they speak of love," and in case we had forgotten, the editors reminded us in a footnote: "Paris in the springtime is for love, as we know." Given the subject of his recent books, we would not have been surprised if Norman Mailer's contribution to the *New York Review*, announced on the cover as "A Vision of Hell," had taken off on the same subject. However, it turned out to be the introduction to *In the Belly of the Beast* by that ill-starred ex-convict, Jack H. Abbott. In it one finds this not very loving statement: "We are all so guilty at the way we have allowed the world around us to become more ugly and tasteless every year that we surrender to terror and steep ourselves in it."

There were moments in Modigliani's last years when he probably would have agreed with Mailer, but it is hard to see the effect of such moments in his paintings, so many of which suggest a man who had not lost faith in an erotic utopia. Thinking of them, not Mailer, my wife and I left that place and walked along the Seine to a point where, on the approach to Pont Neuf and oblivious of the noonday traffic, two clutched-together young lovers had obviously chosen Modigliani over Mailer. But this was not odd for we too had discovered that not only Paris but Europe generally, in the springtime or anytime, was for love of one sort or another, either in present fact or in recollection.

We saw lovers strolling hand-in-hand through the Modigliani exhibit or the Louvre, or ducking under the turnstile in the rue du Bac Métro station and kissing afterward. They kissed between sips of Coca-Cola or Fanta as they sat on the banks of Lac Inférieur in the Bois de Boulougne, or as they stood in line on the Champs-Elysées to see Paul Newman in *Le Policeman*. Young motorbiking lovers startled us with their temerity as they held hands traveling side by side on rue Bonaparte, and young thespian lovers charmed us with their optimism at a Friday evening in Maggi Nolan's Celebrity Services office, where not too many Friday evenings previously the late William Saroyan had charmed everyone. On the train to Paris we shared a couchette with a young couple so intoxicated with one another that they had no need of the Scotch we offered to share with them and seemed unaware that the car, in the best tradition of Italian railroading, had been dispatched from Rome without water and with unflushable toilets.

Goethe wrote of his first experience of Venice that "nowhere does one feel himself more solitary than in a crowd." This is the way it is with lovers also. We saw them in their amorous isolation in Venice among the pigeons and the tourists of all nations in St. Mark's Square, in Rome at the Trevi Fountain, and in the Colosseum. In Siena we saw young lovers kissing as they came hurrying hand-in-hand down the narrow and treacherously cobbled Via di Citta. In the Roman ruins at Fiesole, one of D.H. Lawrence's Etruscan Places, we and other Sunday visitors stepped respectfully around lovers lying abstracted out of time in the long grass—as were those other lovers who lay in one another's arms in the open middle section of Ponte Vecchio in Florence, where the lost children of the world gathered with bedrolls, backpacks, and guitars around the bust of Benvenuto Cellini, himself a proper patron for lovers.

Nobody says that London in the springtime is for love, but even in London there was an ambiance of romance that took the edge off the news of strikes, riots, and IRA starvation in Northern Ireland. It seems to us that when the weather was right, which wasn't too often, lovers lay in the grass in Russell Square in unprecedented numbers. Perhaps the forthcoming royal wedding was a factor. *Paris Match* estimated that 1600 items decorated with pictures of the loving couple were offered for sale in British stores.

Of course, not all love is happy love, as the poets know. Mendicant troubadours sang of lost love in the square in front of the Georges Pompidou Center in Paris, in the métro tunnels and métro trains, and happy lovers contributed to them generously, perhaps out of a realization that happy love can be a good story only when lost love is a possibility. On the steps of the church of San Gaetano in Florence two young lovers—German, we guessed—held hands and cried together, and on the Ponte Vecchio among the lost children of the world a bedraggled girl cried in the arms of a bedraggled boy. Two handsome young Japanese cried with their arms around each other in the Colosseum. In London, the *Sunday Observer* featured somewhat belatedly the lost love of Jean Harris for Dr. Herman Tarnower. Meanwhile, the American musical *Pal Joey*, enjoying a successful London revival, featured the erotic adventures of the aging socialite, Mrs. Vera Simpson, who is "bewitched, bothered, and bewildered" to find herself in love again and happy only when she is in love no more. No doubt D.H. Lawrence, who has left his mark all over Europe, would say of her, as of Jean Harris, that she suffered from sex in the head and was therefore doomed to bewitchment and botheration.

But love in the springtime takes many forms. In Rome we lived near the Spanish Steps, beside which Joseph Severn once nursed the dying Keats and at the top of which, in the opening of Tennessee Williams's *The Roman Spring of Mrs. Stone*, stands that menacing drifter who in due time will possess the aging beauty—who may also suffer from sex in the head. On a newsstand in the Rome railroad station pornography was on display beside *Flash Gordon*, *Walt Disney*, and books by and about the Pope. In the Bargello Museum in Florence, Michelangelo's statue of Bacchus had been rendered perhaps permanently obscene for many viewers because some vandal had broken off its penis. It is not easy to find a McDonald's in Paris, but sex shops are no problem; some of them, as we first noticed in rue des Lombards near the Pompidou, even honor Visa cards. In London's Leicester Square, sex shops were as numerous as electronic games arcades, and Basil Seal was complaining in the *Tatler* that "at a recent count, central Soho contained more than 150 establishments offering some sort of filth." Our copy of *Where To Go: The*

London Guide included a supplementary "Adult guide" that indicated where one might engage Antoinette, Samantha, Sandie, Natasha, Candy, or Natalie (professional virgins retired out of Barbara Cartland romances, perhaps) to escort, pamper, anoint, or massage you (TV lounge and free drinks included) or relax you with "enemas Victorian and modern." In bookstores it was not unusual to find *Charles and Diana: A Royal Love Story* competing for attention with Gay Talese's *Thy Neighbor's Wife*, as if the management had decided that even royal romance could benefit from a second perspective.

One can assume that the Pope looks on Talese's kind of loving as something that belongs in the second circle of Dante's Hell. Indeed, not so long ago the Pope startled the world with the announcement that it was wrong to lust after one's own wife, let alone someone else's—intending, perhaps, to clear up some of the confusion about sexual love that had resulted from the earlier papal announcements on the subject by Wilhelm Reich, Norman O. Brown, and Alex Comfort. In any event, we arrived in St. Peter's Square the Sunday after the assassination attempt in time to hear the Pope say in his taped statement: "I pray for the brother who shot me, and I sincerely forgive him." Appropriately enough, inside the Basilica the Mass of the day began with this prayer: "God our Father, look upon us with love. You redeem us and make us your children in Christ."

The Pope was speaking out of charity, in Christian terms the highest form of love. But the would-be assassin, Mehmet Ali Agca, must be given his charitable due. He had acted out of no personal desire, only a burning need to protest the silence of the world about the hundreds of thousands of victims of Soviet and American imperialism. So he too was a kind of lover—no less than was John Hinckley who devoted his attempted assassination of President Reagan to the movie star, Jodie Foster. Agca's shooting of the Pope, like Dante's love of Beatrice, was only a means to higher things. Indeed, he was a version of that most dangerous kind of lover, the armed idealist. One of his kind, Peter Sutcliffe, "The Yorkshire Ripper," would soon be sentenced in England to life imprisonment for the brutal slaying of thirteen women during a five-year reign of terror, the judge not having been persuaded by the Ripper's argument that he had a divine mission to rid the world of prostitutes.

We remembered Agca in Paris as we visited the prison in the Conciergerie, where in the Chapel of the Girondins you may see such mementos of that earlier Terror as Marie Antoinette's crucifix and a guillotine blade. Danton and after him Robespierre are said to have been detained before execution in one of the small cells opening off the chapel. Robespierre, the incorruptible and passionate lover of the Republic of Virtue, speaks for Agcas and Pol Pots yet unborn when the playwright Georg Büchner has him say in *Danton's Death*: "Vice must be punished. Virtue must rule through the Terror." His utopian vision having been sharpened by the censorship of fanaticism, he can say quite honestly: "The number of scoundrels is not great; we have only to lop off a few more heads and the country is saved." Who would have understood better the words of that armed Libyan idealist, Mu'ammar al-Qaddafi, which we had read the day before in *Time*: "The duty of the revolutionary committee is to practice revolutionary violence against the enemies of the revolution"?

St. Peter's Square—indeed, all of Vatican City—was an exciting place those days. Something had happened. Terrorists, as Walter Laquer has said, are the super-entertainers of our time because "they will always have to be innovative." What greater innovation than to shoot the Pope while he was mingling fraternally with people who were in effect his guests? Of course, most people were sorry for the Pope, and many admired his charitable forgiveness of his brother. But surely there were some who understood very well that brother's kind of loving and secretly sympathized with it, having come to believe (usually from a safe distance) that there is something vital and honest in it that is directed, however extremely and confusedly, against the ugliness of the world that so discourages Norman Mailer.

Keats dying beside the Spanish Steps could only dream of Venice, where Wagner, himself a fabulous lover, finished that fabulous love story, *Tristan and Isolde*. There one day we ate lunch at a standup bar close to where Byron once lived above the shop of a draper, with whose young, dark-eyed wife he promptly began an affair. Indeed, now free from his own wife, "that virtuous monster, Miss Milbanke," he enjoyed various Venetian ladies from one of whom he picked up gonorrhea. Here too he met Countess Teresa Guiccioli and became her faithful *cavalier servente*, a role he continued to play later in Ravenna, where he established himself with his famous menagerie. Yet dying in Missolonghi a few years later it was not his fulfilled love for Teresa that he celebrated in what was probably his last poem, but his unfulfilled love for the handsome Greek boy, Loukas, who had become his page.

D. H. Lawrence, whose *Lady Chatterley's Lover* was written and first published in Florence, defined love in terms of a romantic obliteration of personality, and one consequence is that not only do the women in Lawrence, Byron, and Shelley have a tendency to sound like clones off the same original, but there is a sameness in the language of passionate abandon that they inspire. In their presence we are too often embarrassingly close to the erotic ecstasies of the tabloids and old-fashioned movie magazines. The ecstasy is the problem. To be denied ecstasy in this post-Enlightenment world is to be denied that other prelapsarian birthright, Utopia. The Air Afrique ad in the Paris Métro stations, featuring Ideal Beauty as a seductive girl in a white bikini, offered both at once to all who would fly away with it and her to La Fête du Soleil—there to experience the time-stopping transcendence of what Shelley in "Epipsychidion" calls "passion's golden purity."

The Air Afrique lady may be to us a familiar incarnation of a cultural Muse, but she is not the kind of Muse Etienne Gilson writes about in *A Choir of Muses*. His Muses "are primarily divinities invented by the Greeks to account for the ordered design which confers upon certain of the ideas and works of man a superhuman loveliness." They are "the women who have inspired men to write," for they reveal "the living unity between love, art, and religion." They elicit the demand that all must be sacrificed to the absolute beauty they reveal so that the poet may sing the better. This is the way it was with Dante and Beatrice, about whom we often thought as we walked along Via del Corso in Florence where they may have met, and this is the way it was with Petrarch and Laura, though Petrarch, being more of a modern man, had a harder time putting down his carnal impulses.

In the chill, crepuscular catacombs of the French Pantheon where we went one morning there are great writers enough but Muses are in short supply. Voltaire is there, sharing a place of honor across the corridor from Rousseau, from whose tomb a hand holding a torch protrudes as if a man trapped inside a doghouse were trying to burn his way out. In life at least no love was lost between these two. Rousseau disparaged Voltaire as a playwright, and in an anonymous pamphlet Voltaire called Rousseau a heartless father for having abandoned the bastards produced for him by Thérèse le Vasseur. Voltaire also thought the success of *La Nouvelle Heloïse* one of the infamies of the century. If such sentiments do not suggest a personality so vitriolic no Muse could tolerate it, then his own successful novel *Candide* does. A Muse would have to tend her own garden, not his, and this is not what Muses are supposed to do.

Hugo is there too, sharing a cell with Zola. He loved many women, but none of them qualifies as a Muse—surely not Juliette Drouet who at age twenty-six began a half century's devotion to him as a mistress. She served him as a nurse, secretary, and confidante, in the process writing him 17,000 letters, and tolerated his many infidelities, one of which almost landed him in jail. At her funeral Auguste Vacquerie referred to her as a heroine with "a right to her part in the poet's glory, having shown her loyalty in the time of testing." Hugo's own funeral procession was witnessed by more than a million people, and attended by rolling drums, booming cannons, and twelve wagonloads of flowers. Edmond Goncourt reports in his *Journal* that the women from the brothels had celebrated the occasion the night before with "a tremendous copulation," offering themselves "to all comers on the grass along the Champs Elysées."

Muses tended to disappear in Hugo's century in proportion as the secular spirit made it hard to believe in a love that moves the heavens and all the stars. After Darwin, Marx, Nietzsche, and Freud, potential Muses had to settle for domestic bliss, become call girls, or learn to administer enemas Victorian and modern to narcissistic males who idolized their own passions. Flaubert, for whom the world was as ugly as it is for Mailer, had literature as his idol and thus no more needed a Muse than Joyce did. And it would be a brave Muse indeed who would venture with Lawrence into the dark forests of his soul, which in *Studies in Classic American Literature* he opposes to the lighted clearing in which Benjamin Franklin's "venery" takes place. Certainly Frieda was not his Muse any more than she was John Middleton Murry's, and when the latter two became lovers after visiting Lawrence's grave at Vence one could only hope that the dead man still exercised enough spiritualizing power over both of them to keep their love from being mere venery.

Only the Pope has a Muse that Dante and Petrarch would understand. According to a *Newsweek* we read in Florence, the hospital room in which he lay recovering from his wounds was decorated with a picture of his beloved Black Madonna of Częstochowa. As he lay there, certain personal effects of Marilyn Monroe, including a 36D pink mesh bra, were auctioned off at Southeby's in London. The purchaser of a strapless evening gown promised to resell it later for children's charity—and charity, as the Pope should know, is love.

For Byron, as for so many romantics, the ideal lovers' enclave is an island, where the syphilis that plagued nineteenth-century writers is as unlikely as *Dr. Spock's Baby and Child Care* is unnecessary. This compelling island idea, so closely linked to the idolization of art and sexual love, has its political analogue, as the *International Herald Tribune* kept reminding us while we roamed about Europe. The armed idealists with their fierce and uncompromising charity, and fired with their own kind of passion's golden purity, were just as busy obliterating personality in the interest of their grand schemes as their predecessors were two centuries ago when Western Civilization first became intoxicated with the idea of Utopia and began to experience its tradeoff in disgust with the ugliness of the given world. Now we no more expect negotiable demands from terrorists than we expect true love to be put off by fear of adultery or true art to result if the artist is afraid to sacrifice wife and children to it. Lawrence thought *Ulysses* was a dirty book, but it was the product of the same non-negotiable heroics as his own *Chatterley*. And when was Robespierre, the fanatic idolator of the Republic of Virtue, more their heroic fellow artist than when he refused to be distracted from his grand objective by a squeamish reluctance to chop off a few more heads?

Modigliani, whose paintings speak of love, was of this company. He died of tuberculosis in the nuns' charity hospital on rue Jacob, home street for us in Paris as it had been earlier for Wagner, Sherwood Anderson, and Hemingway. One beautiful Sunday early in June, such a day as makes old lovers young again, we went looking for him in Père-Lachaise cemetery. We found him in the Jewish section in the corner of which is the heartbreaking memorial to those six hundred thousand French who in World War II died for France as deportees in the German work force or as fuel for the ovens of Auschwitz. Modigliani shares the grave with his mistress, Jeanne Hébuterne, she having earned her place, the headstone told us, because in her devotion to him she had made the supreme sacrifice. While a Goodyear blimp, sounding like a distant motorboat on a mountain lake, drifted below cotton puff clouds, we thought of the final act in that sacrifice: her suicidal leap from a fifth-story window in her parents' apartment the morning after Modigliani's death.

Jeanne Hébuterne, says the biographer Pierre Sichel, was Modigliani's only great love. No other woman "would have subjected herself to Modi's whims." She "had the capacity to give herself totally to him," and she "gave gladly, without thinking" for they were "well matched, a perfect couple," all of which makes her sound like a woman Lawrence would have approved of. She gave him one child and was nine months pregnant with another when she died, so her supreme sacrifice may have had some desperation in it. The whims she had subjected herself to had been aggravated by drugs, alcohol, poverty, lack of recognition, and deteriorating health; often he treated her in the best tradition of the totally committed and half-maddened artist, which is to say that he often treated her abominably. "He believed in himself and his art," says Sichel, "and truly, nothing else ever mattered." What

Sichel does not say is that Modi had been anticipated by that political artist, Robespierre the Incorruptible, who never hesitated to offer a few more heads on the altar of the Republic of Virtue.

This willingness of the artist to sacrifice all, including his own mental and physical well-being, on the altar of art guarantees him an authentically eventful biography. This is why we sometimes felt sorry for such part-time Florentines as Hawthorne, Longfellow, and Browning, whose biographies, especially in their love relationships, are so old fashioned—one might even say inartistic. As young men they were not rebellious hell-raisers. They married the women they loved, having courted them properly first, and as husbands they were faithful and loving. They were law-abiding citizens, paid their debts, honored their contracts. They were relatively free from that obsession with the ugliness of the bourgeois that was beginning to validate the lives of literary intellectuals.

Hawthorne, who fought the Florentine mosquitoes with as little success as we did and who once visited the Brownings at Casa Guidi for tea and strawberries, certainly had the wrong biography for Lawrence, just as America had the wrong history. In his cranky if sometimes shrewd study of *The Scarlet Letter* he admires the "blue-eyed darling of a Nathaniel" for having in "perfect duplicity" written the "most colossal satire ever penned" about an America that, being a phallic disaster, cannot know its women darkly in the blood. Lawrence seems to be implying that Hawthorne was so crippled by his culture that he was unable to write an American *Lady Chatterley's Lover*—an implication agreeable to many American readers.

Longfellow was a fine teacher and an important transmitter of European literature to America, as well as a poet whose marvelous ear and instinct for technical experimentation should have impressed Ezra Pound, who was said to be his grand-nephew. But who reads him now? Whenever in Florence we walked by the building in which he had lived on the Piazza di Santa Maria Novella, I thought how unwisely he had ordered his life. If like Lawrence he had run off with someone else's wife, if like Stendhal he had come away from his first sexual encounter with a venereal disease that plagued him the rest of his life, if like Hugo he had remained avid of nymphs into old age, if after the trauma of his beloved wife's accidental death by fire he had become an alcoholic instead of picking up his life like the man of character he was—if he had done at least one of these things we might take him more seriously as a poet today. We might even be tempted to read "Hiawatha" and "Evangeline" as duplicitous surfaces beneath which frustrated dark phallic forces surge.

Sometimes we strolled into Browning's neighborhood near the Pitti Palace, always crossing on the Ponte Vecchio where, it was easy to believe, the lost children of the world were preparing their own brief and sad biographies. Browning was and is a great poet; even Ezra Pound had to live with that fact. He was great without the biographical advantages that have almost become the certain signs of the authentic artist. He loved a splendid woman all the days of their life together and was loved by her in turn, and when she died he was devastated, but being like Longfellow a man of character he picked himself up and went back to being a great poet, which itself suggests a quality of loving about which Byron and Shelley had only heard rumors.

Browning, in any event, made the better approach to the brilliant London revival of *Oklahoma!* which we saw one afternoon as our wanderings came to an end. No doubt, there were far more patrons in the sex shops of Leicester Square that afternoon, submitting themselves to the darkness in their blood, than there were in the Palace Theater. There are those who describe *Oklahoma!* as a sentimental love affair with a lost America, if not an America that never existed at all. But it is *Pal Joey*, which we had seen a few nights before, that is both sentimental and cynical—even Byronic in its denial of the world of true romance in which musical comedy belongs. Romance in *Oklahoma!*, thanks to the inspired collaboration of composer, lyricist, and choreographer, has psychological and moral complexity without ever losing sight of the life-supporting distinction among kinds of loving that characterizes Dante's *Commedia* and Shakespeare's *As You Like It*. Once the pornographic imagination of Jud has been vanquished, we expect the lovers Laurey and Curly to enjoy their honeymoon, their island out of time, but we know that their wished-for destiny is not the utopia of passion's golden purity but life as husband and wife in the human, time-bound community. Basically, one might say, it is a very Victorian story. Byron would have had as much fun with it as the royal wedding had it been available as grist to feed into the mill of his *Don Juan*.

And so then, with Browning and *Oklahoma!* still in mind, to Westminster Cathedral on Trinity Sunday, the day on which is celebrated, as Dante celebrates it in the last canto of the *Commedia*, the divine collaboration of Father, Son, and Holy Ghost—the Holy Ghost whom Lawrence always celebrated, if in terms that would have given little comfort to the now convalescing Pope. Here, depicting their own pageant of love, are Eric Gill's great Stations of the Cross. And here on this day we heard these words from St. Paul's Second Letter to the Corinthians: "Live in peace, and the God of love and peace will be with you. Greet one another with the holy kiss."

What was this if not a charitable injunction to a world confused perhaps no less than ours by the conflicting imperatives of love?

The Fear of Crisis
1985

In the November 1986 *Encounter*, the Princeton University economist Harold James sets out to tell us "Why We Should Learn to Love a Crisis." His explanation is not quite what we would expect from a champion of a market economy. In that economy, he says, crises serve a necessary function; states should not try to avoid them out of a reluctance to risk since they can be purgative and therapeutic; most importantly, small crises may be ideal ways of avoiding major crises.

Professor James stays pretty much within his own discipline, but because he stays there so competently and readably we get the impression that there is much to be said about the relevance of his thesis to the understanding and management of crises generally. Certainly, he will encourage many readers to extrapolate his essay into the worlds of politics and religion. There in more familiar territory they are likely to ask the sort of questions that James's fellow economists may be asking him.

First is the question of scale. It may be that small crises are good for us because they help prevent big crises; but how do we tell them apart when they are happening? Even the layman, for whom economics is, as it was for Carlyle, the dismal science, can see the difference between the inside trading scandals that periodically rock Wall Street and the stock market crash of the early 1930s—especially when Dow Jones quickly indicates that the economy has received no mortal wound from the former. But when we were going through the Iran arms crisis, was it properly identified as major or minor? Where on a scale ranging from Watergate to the discovery that the government had been using disinformation against Libya should it have been placed? The consequence for the nation depended on that placement, and that placement depended on the extent to which we could or could not see it in a perspective of major events since World War II.

The proper placement of a crisis on a proper scale is, of course, crucial in every walk of life at any time. This is no doubt why the literature of crisis management, however called, is as extensive as it is now, when, as it may seem to us Americans, our complex and information-crammed world condemns us to a crisis-rich environment. However, people in any democratic society have a notorious capacity to turn small crises into big ones, to say nothing of a perverse capacity to become addicted to crises of all dimensions. This is in part because crises are relief from boredom, and boredom in democratic societies, where it is easy for the individual to become alienated from boredom-reducing communal structures, is always an important determinant of political and social history. But even apart from such alienation, life in a democratic society, relative to more authoritarian societies, is crisis-oriented by its very nature, which is only to say that in it establishments of power and privilege are constantly and excitingly open to challenge. In such a political environment, a certain dependence on crises is inevitable and even desirable, and the inability often to distinguish between small and big crises is, for better or worse, part of democracy's ongoing effort to remind itself that it is embarked on a precarious enterprise. Perhaps this is why Jefferson once wrote to Madison that "a little rebellion, now and then, is a good thing, and as necessary in the political world as storms in the physical."

Now as always the media make their contribution to the nation's effort to identify itself through the management of crises. The success of a democracy depends on the free flow of information and the capacity of citizens to bear a heavy burden of interpretation—a burden that has increased as the media have multiplied and become more sophisticated. The First Amendment makes the nation crisis-prone, and may have been the Constitution's way of saying what Jefferson in effect said to Madison, that we ought to love a crisis, and perhaps too its way of identifying boredom as a major enemy of democracy.

Since the earliest days of the Republic, the media have been accursed (often enough rightly) of misevaluating crises, either by blowing small ones into big ones or missing the big ones altogether because they developed without newsworthy handles or appeared small because their implications for the future could not be foreseen. This is not that the media are fundamentally irresponsible, biased, or shortsighted, but in considerable part it is that the media, fearing and hating boredom as they do, are themselves crisis-prone. The communicator in any democratic medium is especially free to take into account the strong possibility that his hype-wary audience is listening with only half an ear, is distracted by competing messages with competing interpretations, or is likely for one reason or another to miss the full import of the message. As a consequence, the media resort to those proven boredom-resisting and attention-getting devices of the storyteller, the poet, and the advertiser. As the ancient rhetoricians knew, these devices are not necessarily incompatible with clear and honest communication. If they were, it would be impossible to try to relate the *National Enquirer* to the *New York Times* on a credibility scale, and meaningful communication would be impossible.

Nevertheless, given the proliferation of and competition among the media, it is inevitable that media people will often and rightly be accused of encouraging in the public a misevaluation of a crisis. To judge from such publications as *Pravda, Soviet Life, Soviet Literature,* and *World Marxist Review,* the media of the Marxist-Leninist world should get much higher marks for crisis management. Unhampered by a First Amendment, the party can benevolently assume the burden of interpretation of events and control the crisis scale. Indeed, to judge from such controlled media, the societies they report on do not have to distinguish between big and small crises since such crises that get into print appear small and easily manageable. The big danger, then, is that someone will leak the suppressed truth, as the truth of Gulag was leaked, effecting a major crisis on the French Marxist left.

Those familiar with the excitements of a crisis-prone democratic society may suspect that life in totalitarian societies is a very dull affair, but they fail to take into account the extent to which shortage, privation, and surveillance can compensate for the excitements of a First Amendment. It may be apparent enough from the outside that totalitarian societies suffer from economic, social, and managerial crises, big and small, but within those societies crises tend to be so institutionalized that they cannot be isolated for public scrutiny and divided into big and small. And that which ceases to be subject to division soon ceases to have a public existence. The excitement associated with crisis in a free society thus goes underground and comes out as the thrill of the riskily obtained extra ration of meat or bottle of vodka. Under these circumstances, there is not much chance of learning from small crises.

It is worth noting, however, that Professor James's essay clearly assumes that there is something like a universal wish not to be put in the situation of having to learn from even small crises. There is a sense of fragile all-aloneness in a democracy relative to older and more authoritarian forms of government. Democracies normally begin in a crisis relationship with one of these forms and from that point never cease to be a test of nerve. In these circumstances, a crisis that would be small in a monarchy can be big in a democracy and bring with it the fear of a demoralized return (as has happened often enough in Africa) to an earlier authoritarian condition. Therefore, people in a democracy may experience a particular crisis as exciting, purgative, and therapeutic and yet hope that the last one will indeed be the last one. That "should" in James's title is, after all, only a subjunctive, and inside every subjunctive is an indicative trying to free itself from the clutch of the subjunctive—so that "We should love a crisis" gives way to "There will be no more crises." James's essay is then unavoidably a preachment against the utopian impulse, and an assertion that the desire to get beyond crises can be as great a threat to democracy as it is an exploitable advantage for the indicative totalitarians.

To expect that a democratic society can be crisisless is to expect from it what is commonly expected from religion. Religion is what you are supposed to get when you pass through a crisis experience, after which you are able to observe the crisis-racked secular world with an ironic if charitable equanimity. This is why theocracy, that condition where religion and government have interpenetrated one another, has so often seemed to be the ideal response to the fear of crisis (and why it is the very model of the secularized and crisisless terminal condition that Marx imagined). As we know from our own New England beginnings, theocracies could break up in the big crises that developed during the small crises from which they had learned nothing. However, this development has not kept Americans from identifying the experience of true religion as a crisisless affair.

American democracy, which to exist must find ways to check its utopian impulse, has thus been the spawning ground for religious and pseudo-religious groups in which that impulse, being protected by the Bill of Rights, is free to expand—even to the point where it threatens to break through the barrier separating Church and State. Ironically, that barrier, one of whose aims is to protect democracy from the temptations to theocratic totalitarianism, is itself a generator of crisis. There is ultimately no way to keep religion out of politics—not when the Constitution itself protects religious freedom; nor is there any reason to believe that a democracy would be better off if the barrier were utterly impregnable. If it were, what Richard J. Neuhaus has aptly called the naked public square might soon become a secular wasteland in which the most sinister crisis managers would be free to put into practice their conviction that even the small crises of democracy make politics a thoroughly bad thing.

Protestant Christianity has been in a state of crisis since the Reformation, in the crisis conditions of which it was born. Its genesis has a good deal to do with the multiplication of sects and with the intensification of the conviction, as we see it expressed in 17th- and 18th-century American millennialism, that religion is authentic in proportion as it makes possible here and now, not only in the hereafter, a life beyond crisis. This is the assumption of that rousing millennialist war cry "The Battle Hymn of the Republic," which despite its anti-Catholic origins is now included in many Catholic hymnals.

Catholics can be no less crisis-prone once they are convinced that the authenticity of the Church depends on its capacity to enable the faithful to experience harmonious unity. In this view, crises are what happen when the individual is not sufficiently Catholic—unless they are simply the misidentifications of malevolent outsiders. This attitude had a good deal to do with events in Church history that led up to Vatican II, before which the fear of harmony-disrupting crises made it easy to overlook or misinterpret the small crises from which the Church might have learned how to avoid the big crises that made the Council necessary. Certainly it might have learned that, as Peter Steinfels puts it in "Vatican Wars" (*The New Republic*, December 8, 1986), "a Church that makes large claims is sure to have large problems." And the changes in Church policy made by Vatican II created more crises, not all of them small, for those Catholics who remained attached to the old image of the harmonious Church Universal—so much so that some, in an attempt to get beyond crisis again, cast their lot with such comforting imitations of the pre-Vatican II Church as the Tridentine Latin Rite Church.

But even those who accepted the Council joyfully soon learned that the resolution of some crises caused new ones. For a generation now, Catholics have had to live with the crises caused by birth control, abortion, the position of women in the Church, the celibacy of the clergy, situation ethics, the extent and nature of Papal authority, changes in the liturgy, and liberation theology. Most recently, American Catholics have had to adjust to what proved to be controversial positions of their bishops on nuclear arms and the option for the poor—to say nothing of the cases of Archbishop Raymond Hunthausen and Catholic University theologian Father Charles E. Curran, which have caused tension between the bishops and Rome.

To some American Catholics it is as disillusioning now to find differences of opinion among the bishops, and between them and Rome, as it was to see differences of opinion at work during the Council. Differences of opinion are not only likely to result in crises, but the efforts in the Council to make particular opinions prevail also convinced many Catholics that the Church had become corrupted by that secular evil, politics. This scandalized, if naive, reaction was often enough an indication that such Catholics had a low opinion of democracy, which is nothing if not political, and were at heart as theocratic as the old Protestant millennialists. This attitude, potentially crippling to Catholics in the free world everywhere, not only in America, was vigorously attacked by people like Jesuit John Courtney Murray, who had Chapter 4 of *The Pastoral Constitution of the Church in the Modern World* for support.

In any event, the use of terms native to politics and cultural criticism in an effort to understand conflict of opinion in the Church is by now commonplace. As Peter Steinfels points out, antinomies like liberal/conservative and dissent/authority make it easy to miss the subtleties of a dialectic that is seeking not the triumph of one party over another but a viable center. Nothing could impede such an objective more than a hounding apprehension of the crises that might result if all does not go well. It is this apprehension in secular as well as religious deliberations that so often dictates the censorship, stonewalling, or electronic eavesdropping that only lays the ground for unanticipated crises. It also prepares for the embarrassments institutions must subsequently live with as best they can—for instance, the distinguished philosopher Jacques Maritain not being awarded an honorary degree by the Catholic University of the Sacred Heart in Milan because, in the opinion of a Holy Office cardinal, Maritain was not sufficiently orthodox.

The so-called heresies of Americanism and Modernism at the turn of the century are classic examples of how unanticipated crises can arise when an inordinate fear of crisis takes over in an institution. Analogously, one can see how the crisis-fearing arguments in defense of slavery by intelligent and well-meaning Southerners like George Fitzhugh and Reuben Davis helped to set up a bloody and nation-shaking crisis they never anticipated. On the other hand, when modifications of, or radical departures from, principle, doctrine, or dogma are motivated more by the fear of an unmanageable situation than by a prudent and honest perception of needed change, the consequences may be crises more unmanageable than those one began with. We can see this clearly enough now in the political, educational, moral, and religious effects of countercultural liberation in the '60s and early '70s. That was a time when, in secular or religious terms, the center did not hold. As Steinfels puts it, "The viable center will be more viable if tested by a greater resistance." But nothing weakens the resistance so effectively as the fear of crisis.

No doubt about it, we live in a time of crisis, but we have no reason to believe than human beings ever lived otherwise, or even could without ceasing to be human. To be situated in time is to be crisis-prone, which is no doubt why so much money is spent on such time-transcenders and crisis-resolvers as drugs and alcohol. It may be only pride in our victimization combined with a loss of nerve that makes it sometimes seem that we are specially afflicted, that inscrutable and malign forces have elected us not to be elected to the crisisless condition that everything in us yearns for. Under these circumstances citizens no less than believers are likely to harken back nostalgically to the Age of the Fathers—only to find, as Thomas Paine put it in what he called *The American Crisis*, that the Fathers too were living in a time that tried men's souls.

And so it may seem to one who stands, as I did one beautiful spring morning, on an ancient stone wall in Old Corinth where, I was told, St. Paul once stood as he preached to the Corinthian faithful. There one can see the seven remaining pillars of the Temple of Apollo and the towering Acrocorinth dedicated to Aphrodite, where the thousand sacred prostitutes had their temple. There among the wealthy and luxury-loving Corinthians that fabulous voyager and escape artist stayed a year and a half on his first visit. In the two great letters he wrote back after he resumed his always precarious missionary journeys, he made clear the crisis-structured nature of his efforts to establish a viable center: in prisons often; suffering cold, hunger, and sleepless nights; menaced by robbers; thrice shipwrecked; stoned and lashed; frustrated by dissension and backsliding among the brethren. In Antioch he resisted the authority of Barnabas and even had to administer a public rebuke to St. Peter. Through him large claims were made and large problems resulted, and one of the problems, as the souls of men and women were tried, was the recurring expectation among the faithful that they would quickly be freed from all problems—especially from that crisis-engendering problem of being forced, so often, to seek a viable center while seeing through a mirror in an obscure manner.

It was in this crisis-prone but always hopeful tradition, and most appropriately on the Feast of the Conversion of St. Paul, that Pope John XXIII early in 1959 announced the coming "Ecumenical Council" to the Sacred College of Cardinals.

He was speaking in this tradition too when he wrote later in "Ad Petri Cathedram," his first encyclical letter: "In essentials, unity; in doubt, freedom; in all things, charity." It is hard to imagine a better formula for crisis management, whether of Church or State.

Traveling in Style
1988

n the spring of 1987, as I was preparing to go abroad, there were indications that we might be on the threshold of a period when our thinking about style and the state of the economy would be determined by a preoccupation with quality. George Will had reported that Madison Avenue was thinking along these lines in an effort to stimulate the economically necessary discontent of consumers, who, being quantitatively pretty well off, were giving signs of losing interest in new consumer goods. In the same week that Will's newspaper column appeared, Penton Publications (perhaps sensing early on that all was not well with Dow Jones) took over the entire back cover of *Advertising Age* in order to warn that "it's time we faced up to the problem of American product quality." A week earlier, *Newsweek* had begun its special advertising supplement, "The Quest for Quality," with the keynote assertion that such diverse products as Oscar de la Renta evening dresses, Hermes scarves, and Reebok sneakers have in common "a commitment to quality and all that implies."

A commitment to quality implies, of course, some widely admired characteristics. It is easy to believe that those who put quality first are not gross or avaricious, not insensitive to aesthetics and spiritual values. They remind us of the legendary Brooks Brothers suit, good year after year because impervious to the vagaries of fashion—unlike the flashy sartorial ephemera I was soon seeing in London's New Oxford Street. If such people sometimes appear wasteful, as Beau Brummell might have when in the interest of getting the right crease in his cravat he had to throw on the floor a heap of failures, it is only the side effect of a justifying perfectionism.

Perhaps the California task force that hopes to solve social problems by improving individual self-esteem should concentrate on instilling in people the morale-raising conviction not only that they are themselves exemplars of the highest quality but that they have every right to assert the priority of quality in all circumstances, even when they must choose between life and death. Does one have any more right to condemn the unborn to a life of unacceptable quality than to condemn the already born to bargain-basement jeans and sneakers?

But we can anticipate difficulties if Madison Avenue expects too much from quality as a motivator. Quality too readily implies durability and elitism. The man who bought the Brooks Brothers suit (like the woman who bought a Mainbocher dress) not only expected it to stand up against changes of fashion but was pleasantly, if discreetly, aware of belonging to a special minority freed from the planned obsolescence and the vulgar tyranny of style fluctuation. Brummell, a covert or "cool" dandy who anticipated Mainbocher with his conviction that elegance must be without frills, may have been a boon to the cravat makers, but he probably did less for early-nineteenth-century London clothiers than those fashion-crazy overt dandies whom George Cruikshank was so memorably caricaturing as "Monstrosities."

Indeed, there is a conservatism in the preoccupation with quality that suggests anything but the volatile democratic marketplace. Brummell lived in romantic times (even Byron admired his "exquisite propriety"), but for all his elegance, he was a sartorial and political conservative, on intimate terms with the Prince of Wales and the Duchess of Devonshire. Overt dandyism, a touch of which we can see in Bath's Beau Nash, who made himself stand out by wearing the same white beaver hat every day, was not for him. He would have been appalled by the negative dandyism of the late Andy Warhol, who in his early commercial art and partygoing days, says his biographer Patrick S. Smith, self-consciously cultivated his "Raggedy Andy" look. I expect that a tour of the Brummell section of the Printemps department store in Paris would have left him less than flattered—assuming that the prospect of being searched at the entrance by the terrorist-wary police didn't so offend his aristocratic dignity that he refused even to go in the place. In the perspective of the democratic marketplace he was a snob. A snob, of course, has no doubt of his own high quality and is one kind of standard-bearer, but he is the wrong kind of conservative. Unable to imagine another style of thinking, he is a poor survivor in a changing world where cravats will turn into neckties and finally be abandoned altogether for casually open collars. Brummell, in any event, died broke and alone, even worse off in his old age than Beau Nash had been in the previous century, which suggests that those who stake all on quality must be prepared to live with the fact that it may be its own and only reward. They may exemplify a formula for one kind of heroism, but it is one that threatens to depress rather than elevate the Dow Jones average.

Other complications can arise in a capitalist society when too much is made of quality. We like to believe, on the one hand, that quality can and should be irrespective of price, that a Timex might very well outperform a Rolex. On the other hand, we live in a society that has been schooled to believe that you have to pay for quality, so that a desecration is involved when, as Holly Brubach reports in the May 1987 *Atlantic*, a Mainbocher-designed wedding dress for which the Duchess of Windsor paid $250 in 1937 was soon available as a look-alike at Klein's for $8.90. This was no doubt good news for the fathers of lower-middle-class brides, but it probably intensified their cynicism about the integrity of the capitalist pricing system. William R. Greer remarks in *The New York Times* that "consumers willing to pay as much as $1,500 for a Georgio Armani suit often wonder what they are paying for." In Paris, I was startled to see, in a shop on rue de Castiglione, that a clone of my twenty-dollar American hat was priced at a hundred dollars, while what appeared to be a replica of the 295-franc tie I fancied in Sulka's on rue de Rivoli could be bought farther down the street for 69 francs. Indeed, the repeated discovery of the discrepancy between price and value has the disillusioning effect of the repeated discovery of the discrepancy between the public and private lives of the rich and famous. People like the Greek cynic Diogenes, who dressed in a loincloth and lived in a wine barrel, have found a way to protect themselves from such disillusionment, but the way is bad for business.

A possible conclusion is that the economy might be better off if Madison Avenue continues to stimulate the desire to be in fashion, to foster the appetite for the new. Where change is accepted as a thoroughly trustworthy and creative force, quality is no problem: either it is assumed to be something a change-frightened diehard builds his desperate case on or it is assumed that true quality is itself the product of change when change is generously accepted, as it apparently is by those who admire *Wheel of Fortune's* Vanna White for the infinite variety of her wardrobe. A good place to see the latter assumption at work is in the April 1987 *Rolling Stone*, which surveys rock and punk style between 1967 and 1987 and features an interview with David Bowie. Bowie seems to have had an effect on style in his world comparable to that of Nash on eighteenth-century Bath and Brummell on nineteenth-century London. Bowie himself is represented as moving beyond the often flamboyant and grotesque consequences of his own fashion-plating, even to the point of being preoccupied with his new social concerns, but the prediction is that this "ringmaster of rock style" will continue to be a "prodigy of self-invention" who has no doubt that quality follows change. To judge from the students I saw at Cork's University College, Dublin's Trinity College, the University of London, and the Sorbonne, the Bowie look has had the universalizing effect of Pepsi-Cola, McDonald's hamburgers, and the Latin of the the pre-Vatican II Catholic mass.

The consanguinity of quality and change is equally clear in the April issue of the late Andy Warhol's *Interview*, which is no less a quality magazine than *Connoisseur*. Here, thanks to the synergizing effects of paparazzi and ad agencies, we are in the presence of a mystique of change-driven style untroubled by discrepancies between quality and price. Here, too, is an aura of gnosticism, a sense that we are getting messages from a style-plating microworld graced with special insights and dispensations. Only elite insiders can interpret the iconography, and even for them, the non-elect may suspect, mere words fail, as they fail mystics who attempt to communicate their rapturous encounters. George Marciano's textless two-page ad for Guess?, for instance, is in important respects typical of the whole issue. The environment is a desolate one; a flimsily attired barefoot beauty is holding the left hand of a sinister darkly attired man whose face is hidden by his other hand and the brim of a black and not especially stylish hat. Is he a potential rapist she is trying to seduce? What, the outsider may ask, is the ad trying to sell—her clothes or his or both? Or is it simply trying to dramatize lines from a well-known lyric by the seventeenth-century poet Robert Herrick? "A sweet disorder in the dress/ Kindles in clothes a wantonness"? But insiders probably know in their bones that the ad is not so much trying to sell a product as point it toward its transcendental connections, so that the selling of Marciano's products follows as inevitably as virtuous conduct follows grace.

To judge from the expressions on the faces of models in all fashion magazines, the ability to suggest transcendental connections is commercially indispensable. The models smile sometimes, and very prettily indeed, as they project the heightened states of being that products or services have afforded them, but the more characteristic model expression (see those four most unforgettable women in the Revlon ad) suggests captivation by matters of supernal import, as if a person of exquisite sensibility were on the verge of getting the point of a John Ashbery poem or had just caught a whisper of music from the ninth choir of angels. This is the way the mannequins look in the brilliant five-level display of the work of Christian Dior in the Musée des Arts de la Mode in Paris. The expression on the face of Marciano's seductively disheveled young woman is one of somber, even brooding, bemusement, and if she is thinking about sex, it is in a refining out-of-this-world context. She is no more concerned with the crudities of rape or seduction than the Marlboro cowboy is concerned with the sweaty quotidian details of cattle management.

One rarely senses transcendental connections in the looks of writers and artists, certainly not in the portraits of James Joyce in Dublin's Davy Byrne's bar or in London's National Portrait Gallery. In both figurations he is a benign and un-troubled man who suggests anything but the epical derring-do of *Ulysses* and *Finnegans Wake*. His face is as out of rapport with his cultural meaning as is that of Mikhail Gorbachev in Madame Tussaud's wax museum in London. The photo-graphs on display in the Picasso museum in Paris make it clear that the master had no more ability to model his artistic self than Christian Dior had. I was struck with a 1912 photo of him at his atelier at Sorgues, his expression that of a sadly dream-ing man wondering what he was doing there. Fashion models in the act of modeling have no such doubts. They look like Ulysses in the act of being Ulysses. They assume our willingness to forget that they are mere models, and if we cannot assume it, they come across as mere actors—actors pretending not to be actors—in which case their hypocrisy would undercut the effort to advertise. If we take them at the ad's evaluation, they dramatize legendary states of being in which quality and fashion are totally reconciled, in which time and change have ceased to be threats, have in fact teamed up to produce that time-cheating aesthetic triumph that the work of art is. Style is thus salvation and the stylish life is a life of quality, vulgar though that life may appear to a Cruikshank impressed with the bad taste of the stylish one. Under these circumstances, an ad's explicit references to the quality of a product can strike one as redundant.

Unfortunately, however, there are complications. The very effort to assert change as a beneficent force communicates the old sense of it as a force to be feared and resisted, especially now in a technologically accelerated environment. The fear of change has always had an effect on style, whether for philosophic, aesthetic, economic, political, or religious reasons. The return of the miniskirt, unflattering as it is to knobby knees, to say nothing of its inappropriateness in the decorum of the business world, has alerted some women once more to the tyranny of fashion.

There is a long historical precedent for this reaction, so that one might look back enviously to ancient Egypt, where, as James Lava tells us in *Costume and Fashion*, not only was the mere wearing of clothes a kind of class distinction (slaves and many of the lower classes "went about almost, if not completely, naked") but over a period of three thousand years the changes appear to have been minimal. In such a culture, of course, the tyranny of fashion is still operative; it has simply been absorbed into the cultural control system, as is the case in Orwell's *Nineteen Eighty-four*.

This has hardly been the case in Western civilization, but throughout most of the Christian period the consequences of fashion-consciousness have more often than not been railed against by preachers, satirists, and economically pinched rulers. One wonders what Elizabethan satirists would have done for a subject if it hadn't been for the absurdities and extravagances of male, and especially female, attire. Social critics, Elizabeth Burton writes in *The Pageant of Elizabethan England*, "complained that wives now dressed so grandly that they could not be distinguished from fine ladies." Privately Queen Elizabeth might dress plainly enough, but her wardrobe consisted of "3,000 gowns and 82 wigs of different colors." Anne of Cleves, anticipating Vanna White, astonished the court by appearing in a magnificent new dress every day. Vanities of this kind scandalized people like the preacher William Harrison, who wanted a return "to good, old-fashioned dark and suitable attire." One can imagine his reaction to the miniskirts so abundantly displayed that May of 1987 on the streets of Paris—to say nothing of that refinement in beachwear, the stuck-on bikini, he might have seen had he attended the movie festival at Cannes.

Inevitably, governments attempted to curb the appetite for the fashionable and delectable, or shift it in desired directions, by sumptuary legislation. The Romans at one time even tried to limit the number of guests at a feast. In fourteenth-century England, Edward III reacted to wasteful extravagance by ordering that all people restrict themselves to two courses at table. His later regulations prescribed dress according to social rank. Esquires of a certain income, for instance, were not supposed to wear furs, but wives of squires of a higher rank were permitted to wear fur trimmed with miniver. Toward the end of the sixteenth century, everyone over the age of seven was supposed to wear a cap made of English wool, unless the head of the family had an income of over twenty marks a year from land. The satirists, conservative as always, flayed extravagantly dressed middle-class women not only because of their wasteful vanity but because of their violations of decorum. One can imagine the satirist John Marston's response to the news I picked up in London's National Portrait Gallery: that the Duchess of Windsor's jewels had been available to the highest bidder, regardless of rank, at Sotheby's auction in Geneva. If the established iconography of dress was not honored, nobility could not be distinguished from commoners nor the court from the city. Suppose that every rich merchant's Madame insisted on her right to a beauty bath of milk laced with wine in imitation of Mary Queen of Scots?

Sumptuary restrictions and discriminations strike us now as both high-handed and economically ill-advised. Imagine a law that permitted designer jeans for the millionaire class but mandated plain jeans for the rest of us, or a law that made it impossible for a teenage cocaine entrepreneur to discard his ten-speed bicycle and drive about in a Mercedes. In the past, however, sumptuary thinkers expressed a concern not only with conserving scarce materials but with preserving the good order of society. In their own way they were putting quality of life ahead of fashion, as was the British Parliament when, in 1770, it decreed that any woman who "shall seduce or betray into matrimony any of his Majesty's subjects, by the scents, paints, cosmetic washes, artificial teeth, false hair, Spanish wool, iron stays, hoop, high-heeled shoes, bolstered hip" would be considered to have practiced witchcraft and the marriage would be invalidated.

Quality of life is also an issue when sumptuary laws have a moral or religious provenance, as in the old Catholic Lent or the Muslim Ramadan, or a patriotic provenance, as in World War II America when nylon stockings were replaced by leg paint. But it was also the issue in Stalin's Russia, Hitler's Germany, Mao's China, and Pol Pot's Cambodia, where sumptuary regulations mandated the ruthless elimination of vast numbers of people. In such places, a style of Lenten privation was the consequence of a principled disregard of the human person coupled with a faulty economic theory (factors that have proven historically to be synergistically well mated), but it is a style that has often enough seemed indispensable to a utopian pursuit of equality. No doubt this is why when defenders of the Spartan austerities in Marxist societies criticize the fashion-driven consumerism of the Western democracies, they often sound like Elizabethan satirists, if not like that Roman satirist and ferocious misogynist, Juvenal, who believed that the pursuit of luxury, especially by women, was the cause of all evil. Juvenal might have done well in Khomeini's Iran, where women go decorously veiled and Revlon's most unforgettable women are utter nonentities, though he might miss the luxuries he was himself accustomed to. Even worse for his peace of mind, he might discover the extent to which his diatribes were, like Baccarat crystal and Rolex watches, indulgences for an elite that was about as likely to take them seriously as it was to give up its own hard-won perquisites.

Elites, whether jet-setters, leather-and-chain bikers, Greenwich Village or Bloomsbury bohemians, or the Fortune 500, generally imply a wistful attachment to sumptuary restrictions as they attempt to reserve for themselves the distinctions of dress, style, behavior, and language that have the effect of morale-reinforcing indicators of quality. A free society finds it hard to give legal support to such attempts. Elites, consequently, are left with little more than a desperate hope that some residual sense of decorum will protect their identity: that figures like John Gotti, reputed leader of the Gambino crime family, will have the decency not to confuse the social categories by dressing like fashion-conscious captains of legitimate industry. Hence, there are people who are less offended by the way crack-dealing Los Angeles teenagers get rich than by the social disrespect they display in their affluent life-style. They are like those insurgents who, during the Peasants' Revolt in Germany, insisted on their right to wear red clothes like their aristocratic betters. Even executions can violate a decorum that traditionally favored elites: during the French Revolution, for instance, the meanest citizen had the right to be dispatched by guillotine, an instrument previously reserved for aristocratic malefactors.

Elites in democratic societies might appear to inhibit the free development of the capitalist marketplace (which must operate on the assumption that the more eight-hundred-dollar suits or expensive sports cars people can be persuaded to buy the better), but as a matter of fact, they cannot exist satisfactorily on their own terms without becoming cultural fashion plates for the non-elite. Thus a liberated Bloomsbury dissipates its moral capital by encouraging a vulgar repetition of itself in the uptight middle class, so that the latter tends to become less and less inclined to play its part in maintaining Bloomsbury as an affordable luxury for a few. Thus the identifying haute couture of the rock-punk world is threatened by upward vulgarization as it filters into the bourgeois marketplace. Meanwhile, any hoodlum's moll is free to wear Garrard jewelry, douse herself with Catherine Deneuve's perfume, and drink Dom Perignon champagne out of crystal that, as the Baccarat ad assures her, has been "at the service of monarchs, luminaries, statesmen and mere perfectionists."

Theoretically, Marxist societies are liberated from the structural need of elites and the consequent stylistic fluctuations that stand in the way of a truly quality society. As we know, however, these societies have discovered that they cannot function without an elite of top dogs in whose interests sumptuary restrictions, even if only implied, are as important as they were to medieval aristocracy. The wonder is how little resentment they arouse in the unprivileged masses, as if the very existence of such elites has the morale-sustaining function of fashion-plating a possible future. Thus the stylish and glasnosting Gorbachevs are perhaps sources of both pride and hope for the millions who know only the drab uniformity of year-long Ramadans. Having assumed some of the function of a Soviet Madison Avenue, however, they only intensify the opposition of those "Pamyat" ultraconservatives who are reacting to glasnost the way Elizabethan satirists reacted to all those uppity middle-class wives.

The Pamyat reaction should remind us once more that no attempt to spiritualize fashion by equating it with quality is likely to co-opt the ascetic impulse to despise the style-conscious world lest one perish with it. Monks dwelling in desert caves or perched on top of low-rent pillars, eccentric bachelors living deep-thinkingly in wilderness cabins, counterculture hippies communing with the infinite in cold-water pads, disillusioned ex-Manhattan yuppies trying to scratch a bare living from the inhospitable soil—all dramatize the message that the truly quality life demands freedom from, if not militant hostility to, the fashionable marketplace. They scorn not only designer jeans but sometimes plain jeans as well: loincloths or honest nudity are often enough. Something of their spirit (prudently tempered by the ethos of an affluent society) appears in our own new Puritans, who discipline their bodies and deny their impulses in an effort at self-transcendence often equal to that of the early Christian troglodytes. Fortunately for the time- and change-bound marketplace, however, what the economy loses at one end, it often gains back with compound interest at the other: seventy-five-dollar Nike running shoes, special diets, and the membership costs of health clubs can make it expensive to be a New Puritan. But if the romance of creaturely self-abnegation has an ascetic surface, it also has (as was the case with that Old Puritan, Thoreau) an Epicurean rationale. Dr. Kenneth Cooper, whose 1968 book, *Aerobics*, has been so influential in the cult of fitness, has said: "The reason I exercise is for the quality of life I enjoy." In his own way he is helping to make quality fashionable—like Beau Brummell, even helping to counter the ascetic that capitalist consumption is a vulgar and immoral state of affairs.

The impulse toward the new, the untried, and the unconventional that invests the tyranny of fashion with its promise of new and abundant life is widely identified as a romantic one. In *Punch*, for instance, Stanley Reynolds was identifying rock music as a continuation of the Romantic Movement's hostility to the Gentility Principle, and authentic for that reason. To him, the vital and establishment-offending vulgarity of Wordsworth, Byron, and Shelley was the grand precedent for the Beatles, the Rolling Stones, and the Velvet Underground. But in the same week, one could learn from Lise Hand in the Irish *Sunday Independent* that the old romantic pomp and circumstance of formal balls have returned with the sanctioning assistance of Yves Saint Laurent and Ungaro, while on the front page of *The Sunday Times* in London, Harrods was announcing the return of the hat—soft, triumphant, gauzy, and "decidedly romantic."

But those who do not understand romanticism's minimalizing tendency to return to the past, both for inspiration and for protection from the excesses of its own venturesomeness, miss something many of us value highly in the work of Wordsworth, Coleridge, Byron, and Keats. Reynolds saw Mick Jagger as "some sort of legitimate extension of Percy Bysshe Shelley," but if we take Cambridge scholar George Watson's word for it, an increasingly conservative Shelley would in the last three or four years of his short life have given about as much comfort to Jagger as Matthew Arnold would. Indeed, the history of romanticism makes it clear that little in life is as predictable as the cybernetic response of sumptuary restriction to extravagant release. Since the pattern works both ways, it is quite possible that today's New Puritan will, in an effort further to realize his human potential, become tomorrow's New Sybarite. But it is no less possible that the stuck-on bikini, perhaps having become unstuck in too many embarrassing circumstances, will go the way of the stuck-on beauty patch, possibly to be succeeded by the romantic return of the kind of swimsuit in which the aquatic movie star Esther Williams once looked so wonderful.

The minimalizing impulse expresses the fear that unless we cut back, hold fast to what has been proven reliable, we will not only waste scarce resources but we will be unable to brake our movement toward the silence of those infinite spaces that terrified Pascal. This enduring fact puts the marketplace in a bind between durability and fashionableness, and prompts it at times to make as much as it can out of the paradox that less can be more. The Paris weekend magazine *V. S. D.* featured on one of its springtime covers "Immortelle Rita Hayworth," but for at least some readers the stylish late late-movie star was no more immortal than the no less stylish beauties they might have seen in Gerald L. Brockhurst's "Dream of Fair Women" exhibition in London's national Portrait Gallery. No doubt this now all-too-commonplace realization has something to do with the success of Samuel Beckett's plays (an aesthetic of reduced expectations is bound to be welcome in a hype-bedeviled culture) and the continuing popularity of E. F. Schumacher's *Small Is Beautiful.* But it also has something to do with the minimalizing restriction of attention and the maximalizing of available energy that made England's survival in World War II possible—a relationship powerfully memorialized now (with the recorded accompaniment of air-raid sirens and Winston Churchill's rhetoric) in the spartanly styled Cabinet War Rooms in London.

The enduring attraction of the uniform also testifies to the tenacity of the minimalizing impulse and the suspicion behind it that the individual's wasteful need to be stylishly different is a threat to communal life. Uniforms can of course be tastefully and expensively done and proudly worn, whether by Marines, doormen, airline pilots, or Paris policewomen, who look splendid in their blue outfits. Mainbocher, Ms. Brubacher reminds us, designed uniforms for the Waves and the Girl Scouts. Even romantic maximalists like Charles Reich and D. H. Lawrence had high hopes for uniforms: in *The Greening of America* those who have been saved by the counterculture revolution from the technological hell of America all wear jeans, and Mellors, the gamekeeper in *Lady Chatterley's Lover*, populates his ideal society with men wearing "close red trousers, bright red, an' little short white jackets." But even as they were writing, it was becoming clear to other idealists that uniformity might be the only way to harness maximalizing and utopia-threatening individual-ism. Thus, romantics like Reich and Lawrence, who came on as welcome threats to the Gentility Principle, were closer to the sumptuary restrictions of socialist unifor-mitarianism than their admirers realized. An instinctively minimalizing observer might wonder how many of the style-conscious young people he sees in London's New Oxford Street or Paris's Place St. Michel might happily don Mellors's red trousers, or even William Harrison's dark and sensible attire, in the expectation of realizing some guru's dream of communal fulfillment. No doubt many might, but there is some comfort in the profusion of individual variations on the general pattern. Rock and punk styles, which encourage the dandy impulse to express itself to the point of extravagant eccentricity, foster at least the illusion of individuality—and where the individual has a chance, so has democracy.

In the meantime, there are those other minimalizers for whom the tyranny of fashion presents a demoralizing vision of contemporary reality, and who oppose to it a familiar Rousseauean myth of the primitive: the human being before civilization divided his consciousness with anxieties of style and doubts about the quality of his life. But we have another and related myth of the primitive as a reserve of spiritual strength and wonder, to which we can return romantically to enhance our own impoverished and distracted lives. Hence on a gloomy Tuesday late in May, Liz Smith was informing her faithful in *The* (London) *Times* that the flamboyance of African tribal ornamentation was back in style, its voodoo working potent magic on bangles, bracelets, necklaces, and earrings. And in the Picasso museum on an even gloomier Tuesday, it was not easy to forget how sensitive Brancusi, Braque, Modigliani, and Picasso himself were to this potent magic.

Everything we know about the primitives suggests that Picasso was closer to the truth about them than Rousseau was. Wherever we find them, they modify their appearance to raise their morale: hang rings from their ears or put plugs in them; file their teeth; distend their lips with disks; tattoo, paint, and scarify their bodies; pattern their clothing. Human nature, apparently, is as coterminous with a sense of style as with a need of community. This means not only that a headhunter in darkest Africa can within the limits of his means become a dandy, provided that he is not the last man in his tribe, but that if Beau Brummell were left alone with his entire wardrobe on a desert island, he would very quickly stop worrying about the crease in his cravat. To be truly human you cannot be alone, and within the human community, for better or worse, style is the identifier.

The Shakespeare who wrote *King Lear* lets the aged king make this point in Act II, when the evil sisters, Regan and Goneril, are trying to deprive him of the hundred retainers who attend him as he moves about in the kingdom he has retired from. When Regan wonders why he needs even one retainer, Lear exclaims bitterly:

> O reason not the need! Our basest beggars
> Are in the poorest things superfluous.
> Allow not nature more than nature needs,
> Man's life is cheap as beast's.

He has not yet experienced the full import of this protest, as he will in the next act, when he learns the real nature of "unaccommodated" man, but the later experience only underlines its truth. Without an identifying style, Lear, like the rest of us, can no longer be human.

Style, alone, we can infer, will not save us, may even damn us, and at any moment our chance for salvation may hinge on a qualitative change of style, but without style there may be nothing to save. The fact that most of us know this in our bones is why Madison Avenue and the marketplace will probably get along well enough if they continue to assume that fashion is ruled by a benevolent tyrant.

ℳodernism and 𝒥ts 𝒞onsequences
1989

odris Eksteins's disturbing and fascinating book *Rites
of Spring* ranges between the Sergei Diaghilev-managed
opening night performance of Stravinsky's *The Rite of
Spring* in Paris on May 29, 1913, and the suicide of Hitler
in 1945. The book's field of action is Western Civilization, but
its primary focus is on Germany between the two World Wars. Its prologue is set in
Venice where the death from cholera of the artist Gustav Aschenbach in Thomas
Mann's *Death in Venice* prepares for the book's thematic concern with the "colossal
romanticism of our era" in which life has been subordinated to art.

Rites of Spring is thus a book about the hubris of modernism and the consequence of its search "for the holy grail that is the 'total art form.'" In Germany, "the
modernist nation *par excellence* of our century," the search was fueled, Professor
Eksteins says, by the sibling relationship between avant-garde and storm trooper in
which "Nazi kitsch may bear a blood relationship to the highbrow religion of art
proclaimed by many moderns."

Eksteins's decision to present his material in the form of a drama divided into
acts and scenes is an attempt to find a compromise between history and fiction in
an era when existence has become aestheticized. He risks, of course, the very
consequence of blending life with art that is his subject. But he knows what he is
doing, and most importantly, he knows that he is not simply attacking the aesthetic
dimension of reality. One might say that he clarifies history by a discriminate use of
the weapons of an adversary whose totalistic commitment to a regenerating novelty
is, like Diaghilev's or Hitler's, a rejection of history.

The first act gives us the prologue to World War One in Paris and Berlin and the unanticipated appalling fact of it in Flanders Field—if anything, made more appalling by the spontaneous Christmas truce of 1914. The second act carries us through the war to the point where "modernism, which in its prewar form was a culture of hope, a vision of synthesis, would turn to a culture of nightmare." The third act, which begins in Paris on May 21, 1927, with the arrival of Charles Lindbergh ("The New Christ"), concludes with the *liebestod* marriage of Hitler and Eva Braun in the Fuehrer's bunker and the frolicking *danse macabre* that followed in the chancellery canteen when it was clear that the Fuehrer was dead.

So the story of the modern world between May 29, 1913, and May 28, 1945, is the now familiar story of a passage from euphoria to disillusion, a passage almost compulsively repeated in the art of modernism and postmodernism. Paul Fussell has had his say on this subject in *The Great War and Modern Memory*; indeed, readers who know Fussell's book will have it constantly in mind as they read Eksteins's first two acts. Fussell is also good on the aestheticization of war, as among others is Paul Johnson in *Modern Times*. But there is no redundancy here. These books complement one another. This is apparent, for instance, in Fussell's and Eksteins's treatment of Eric Remarque's *All Quiet on the Western Front*. Eksteins, one might say, repeats what Fussell says about the expression of disillusionment in Remarque's novel, but his more extensive concern (Fussell confines himself to the British experience on the Western front during World War One) is with the novel as a reflection of the political and emotional postwar environment that makes it a factor in the rise of the Third Reich.

Other unmentioned books surface as one reads. No doubt the dramatic structure invites this reinforcing invasion of apparently disparate texts, just as Shakepeare's *Macbeth*, with its dramatic progression through murderous totalitarianism to nihilistic despair, now invites the reaffirming invasion of *Rites of Spring*. A good deal of Elias Canetti's *Crowds and Power* becomes relevant, particularly in its treatment of the figure Canetti calls the "Survivor," for whom the piles of dead before him are aesthetically indispensable to his self-enhancement. Eksteins's powerful emphasis on the millenarian impulse in German culture prior to both wars (to say nothing of the utopian expectation of a revolutionary renewal released by modernism in France and England as well) can remind one again how much there is in Norman Cohn's *The Pursuit of the Millenium* that must not be forgotten, especially in its chapter on the medieval heresy of the Free Spirit with its "elite of amoral supermen," those ecstatically liberated souls whose profound introversion could emerge as "a nihilistic megalomania." Indeed, Cohn provides the historical precedent for a Fuehrer who, says Eksteins, "looked on himself as the incarnation of the artist-tyrant Nietzsche called for."

"The notion of regeneration and rebirth," Eksteins writes, "was to be found in much avant-garde activity at the turn of the century." Martin Green has opened out this generalization in his *Mountain of Truth: The Counterculture Begins–Ascona, 1900-1920,* a book that could serve as a prologue to *Rites of Spring.* Inevitably, some of Green's characters appear in Eksteins's book, notably Mary Wigman, whose dance theories interested Albert Speer, and Rudolf von Laban, the ballet master of the Russian state theaters. For Laban the dance was the total art form that in Eksteins's book it is for Diaghilev, who as "a Nietzschean creation, a supreme egotist" anticipates the supreme impresario that Hitler was.

For both Green and Eksteins the priority of the aesthetic, especially when it is in combination with the liberated erotic, foreshadows the counterculture of the 1960s. Summarizing the intellectual and artistic ferment of the 1930s, Eksteins observes that "all these experiments seemed to capture the mystique of the avant-garde movements of an earlier day: to embrace life, to rebel against bourgeois sterility, to hate respectable society, and above all to revolt—to bring about a radical revaluation of all values." In World War One, he tempts us to say, the Germans were a New Left movement on fire with ideas of newness, regeneration, and change, while the British were a conservative and materialistic establishment imprisoned in the past. The shattering reversal of expectation that Germany experienced as it passed from the euphoria of August 1914 to the bitter aftermath of the Versailles Treaty is repeated in the declension of the Haight-Ashbury Summer of Love to the Charles Manson case.

Manson himself was in many ways a reprise of the Hitler he admired: each was a failed artist; each was a charismatic and aesthetic unifier who managed to convince others that through him they belonged in an elite of amoral supermen; each had a compelling vision of a Reich that needed only to be purified by a Final Solution to stand like an embodied total art form against a pusillanimous and visionless world order.

Eksteins speaks of the German "preoccupation with the administration of life, with technique, to the point where technique becomes a value and an aesthetic goal, not merely a means to an end." In Germany, unlike Britain, technical and vocational training was a matter of national and state concern well before World War One. In Hitler's Germany the blending of aesthetics and technique in radio, film, and the meticulously planned Nuremburg spectacles was indispensable to the Third Reich's tyranny of harmony. It was no wonder that Lindbergh's astounding achievement in 1927, representing as it did a Nietzschean triumph of will and technology, should be followed by his idolization in Nazi Germany, where Hermann Goering pinned on him the Service Cross of the German Eagle.

The admiration was mutual: Lindbergh viewed the western democracies as degenerate and incapable of competing with Germany. Later, as a prominent member of the America First Committee, he announced in an angry speech that "the three most important groups who have been pressing this country toward war are the British, the Jewish, and the Roosevelt Administration." His belief that fascism was the wave of the future, Eksteins reminds us, was reflected in Anne Lindbergh's 1940 book *The Wave of the Future* (and shared, apparently, by the young Paul De Man.)

Eksteins's book arrives on the scene at a time when it appears to some observers that there are still New Wave diehards who dream of a Germany capable of being a salvational force in a troubled and divided Europe. Daniel Johnson in the April, 1989 *Encounter*, for instance, calls attention to Arnulf Baring's recently published *Our New Megalomania: Germany Between East and West* with its warning that the new vision "is beginning to resemble the old, fatal German sense of mission, the tragic destiny which already clouded so many first-rate minds in World War I." In a similar vein, Gordon Craig in the June 15, 1989 *New York Review of Books* has compared the ideas of Jean-Marie Le Pen's xenophobic French National Front to the aspirations of the German Right, especially as it is being agitated by the writings of Franz Schoenhuber and his leadership of the right-wing Republican party.

Unsettling thoughts (to close on a personal note) to carry with one to the concentration camp at Dachau on a beautiful Sunday afternoon after high mass at the splendidly resurrected *Frauenkirche* in Munich. But perhaps after all it is the best place to take them. Dachau is a memorial, not a museum, I was advised, and the choice of words is right: in a museum one expects to find a past that is over and done with, easily available to the softening nostalgia of le *temps perdu*. A memorial is for that which in the interests of present and future must be refused such comfortable neutralization.

So one contemplates the appalling photographs and incineration ovens as memorials of a technical efficiency whose culmination in this place was the aestheticization of death. Here the Carmelite nuns have established their prayerful *Karmelkloster*, a memorial, as their founder and first prioress put it, of "what happens when the state becomes the substitute for God." So when the great doomsday bell sounds over the camp at three o'clock one may go into their chapel and hear the nuns recite their memorial office.

Eksteins's book begins with a memorial return to Verdun by way of two cemeteries: first, an automobile graveyard piled high with "smashed corpses, crumpled bodies, glistening skeletons," then that other cemetery where beneath symmetrical rows of white crosses lie those who fell in the battle of Verdun in the Great War. His book, he says, "will try to show that the two graveyards are related." In the process he shows that Dachau is part of the relation.

Traveling in Crowds
1992

ome people, like the Greek cynic Diogenes or the pillar-dwelling St. Simeon Stylites, can't stand crowds at all. Others, like Thoreau or George Bernard Shaw, can stand them only if they are willing to sit still and be lectured to as docile audiences. Most of us, however, have mixed feelings about crowds. We enjoy being in a crowd and benefit from its synergism if we can share its interest: it is better to see a play in a full theater or to watch the Superbowl from the stands, since then we can sense ourselves to be among benevolent co-spectators, not lost in a crowd. When this is not the case a crowd may simply be the anonymous other, a noisy bore that restricts our freedom of movement, distracts our attention, or even terrifies us the way Pascal was terrified by his vision of infinite spaces.

In any event, modern city life is a crowded affair and we learn early to depend on habits of evasion in order to minimize the inconveniences and threats of crowdedness. But the comfortably patterned life of home can become a humdrum that some of us travel to escape, quite confident that our proven ability to live with home crowdedness will stand by us in foreign circumstances. This expectation is likely to stay with us no matter how often we sally forth and discover that it must be qualified; if it did not, our first experience of alien crowdedness would probably be our last. Hence the attraction of the packaged tour group, which has many of the advantages of a visit to the zoo when we have absolute confidence that the cages will contain the animals. The threat of any crowd, foreign or domestic, is that its anonymity will prove infectious. Life in the tour group promises benevolent support as you stand out in a crowd: no one who steps confidently from a luxury coach at the Louvre, Notre Dame, or Westminster Abbey will ever think of himself as anonymous.

But our own benevolent group (mother, father, eldest son), having set out for Europe on its own, quickly discovered, as such amateurs usually do, that it is not the size of a crowd that matters but the context of time and place in which it occurs. If at the Seattle airport you need to ask a crucial question about connections for Rome at Heathrow, the ten people between you and the clerk at the starting gate are a greater threat to your peace of mind than will be those 370 others with whom you will share the 747 for the next nine hours. Those others will affect you as a crowd only when they come aboard and compete for storage space in the overhead bins, or later when too many of them want to use the toilets at the same time. Otherwise they are not a crowd but your fellow passengers whose anonymous presence defines and protects your privacy, which is what any crowd can do if you can keep a safe distance from it. I can work on a book review in a jumbo jet, but never in a bus, train, or commuter plane. In fact, the comfortable privacy of the 747 can trick you into believing that once you arrive crowds will continue to be no problem.

But Heathrow, like any large international airport, can be a rude awakening. Perhaps after blundering around in Terminal One you are standing in front of a screen listing arrivals and departures—Rome, Athens, Budapest, Nice, Belgrade, Zurich, Luxembourg, Hamburg, Paris, Munich, Lyon, Istanbul—and what before were abstractly glamorous places on the map are now the crowded and ego-diminishing immensity of a world in which all strategies of crowd-evasion will ultimately fail. But in Rome the subway can be a more immediate threat to your need to feel in charge of your life. Here, as the desperate getters-on collide with the desperate getters-off, is the perfect image of the crowd as a haphazard coming together of individuals, each of whom is in a hurry and selfishly motivated. Long gone now is the civility of the Paris Métro or the London tube.

Totalitarian dictators hate such spectacles; in fact, they are suspicious of all gatherings that are not informed with politically correct and self-abnegating motivations and try to keep them from forming. With good reason, they fear the destructive uses to which their potential synergy can be put, even if they are only disaffected Muscovites standing in line for scarce potatoes. To a Chinese apparatchik, the Roman subway would have another Tiananmen Square written all over it, and might help him understand why the Italians were having such a hard time organizing a government. Thus the Soviets and the German Democratic Republic once had high hopes for those crowd-dispersing agencies, the KGB and the Stasi. No doubt they would have agreed with the once popular American humorist, Ogden Nash, that people taken one at a time are often very intelligent. Let two or more gather clandestinely together and subversion, not establishment-endorsed common sense, is likely to be the consequence.

From the point of view of a KGB or a Stasi, for whom the individual is always a menace, there are simply too many people, whether they are afoot, on motor cars, bicycles, motor scooters, or inline roller skates. The harassed traveler, trying to board the Roman subway in circumstances when the familiar strategies of crowd evasion prove useless, is likely to agree. Indeed, "crowd" in its most familiar connotation suggests not only that there are too many people generally but that something ought to be done about it. I suspected, as I kept in touch with the larger world through *The International Herald Tribune*, that this was the connotation of the word that delegates to the forthcoming "Earth Summit" in Rio de Janeiro would bring with them. I don't know whether Paul Erlich, author of *The Population Bomb*, ever rode the Roman subway, but if he did he might have seen it as the perfect model of humanity's capacity to crowd itself out of existence. For him population growth must be stopped as soon as possible: families everywhere should be restricted to 1.8 children each, though one must concede that this is still four-fifths of a child more than the goal of the Chinese communists. In America at the present moment there is no announced goal; however, our annual 1.6 million abortions might seem to imply one.

But other efforts to reduce objectionable crowdedness came to our attention as we moved about Europe's sweet springtime. In Yugoslavia the Serbs were embarked on what they called a cleansing operation against the Muslim residents of Bosnia, who with their ethnic and religious otherness were as much a polluting crowd to the Serbs as they were to the Catholics in Marseilles. The Iraqi were trying to enlarge their *lebensraum* by culling out the Kurds. Even the Gypsies, the victims of one of Hitler's cleansing operations, were in short supply in the Paris Métro tunnels. I wondered if they were now victims of the bias against immigrants in the Western democracies, all of which seem to agree with The Federation for American Immigration Reform that they badly need "a temporary moratorium on immigration."

Indeed, there are times when passport travelers with money to spend can themselves be made to feel like immigrants. When, for instance, my very sportily

dressed wife and son paused at the entrance of the Ritz in Paris, the doorman
looked at them as if they were a couple of Yankees who should never have left
home. Conspicuous among the teacher-led band of youngsters I saw behind Notre
Dame cathedral was one who wore a Los Angeles Rams T-shirt. The Ritz doorman
might have looked askance at him too, but he was no longer anonymous, having
discovered early in life that one of the chief functions of style is to make one stand
out in a crowd. This, of course, is why some immigrants get into trouble to begin
with: their strange styles make them stand out when all they want to do is assimilate
comfortably into a new crowd and share its life.

But individuals as well as societies need ways of evading the anonymity of
crowds, however attractive and socially useful that anonymity may sometimes be. In
Paris at the Arc de Triomphe a pavement plaque announces that *"ici repose un
soldat"* who died for his country in World War I. He is an anonymous *"un"* in an
honorific sense, standing for all those others who, dying *"pour la France,"* make not
a crowd but an honored community. On the right-hand wall as you enter the grand
Benedictine church of St.Germain Des Pres the memorial is more particular: ten
banks of names for World War I and four for World War II, all *"morte pour la
France."* Not too far away in the Consiergerie on the Ile de la Cité there are five
other banks of names, *"Liste Générale et Très Exacte"* of those who—with an assist
from the guillotine—died *"pour la France"* in the Reign of Terror. Their particular
and *"très exacte"* being-in-the-world, no less than that of *"un soldat"* at the Arc, was
sacrificed to the nation's fear that its past, if examined in cold blood, might prove to
have been nothing but the Brownian movement of a crowd.

Robespierre, himself listed there as *"ex-deputé à la Convention,"* gets much of the
credit for the cleansing operation that the lists remember. Anyone who aims as
single-mindedly as he did at a Republic of Virtue is likely to end up a population-
reducer. I thought of him as I sat in rue de Buci—one of those splendid places in
Paris where you can be comfortably alone in a crowd—and sipped café au lait as I
read in the *New Yorker* about the population-reduction practices of Cambodia's
Khmer Rouge. Perhaps their charismatic leader Pol Pot only wants what in his terms
is a Republic of Virtue and is just as determined as Robespierre and St. Just were to
thin out the madding crowds that obstruct him. Two days later (now we were in the
air again heading for Chicago on the first leg of a long flight back to the sweet
humdrum of home) I was reading about King Hassan II of Morocco in *The
International Herald Tribune.* He was urging Libya's Mu'ammar al Qaddafi to give up

the terrorists he was accused of harboring. "Politics is not the art of choosing between good and better," the King said, "but between bad and worse." Sell this philosophy to travelers and they will probably prefer the Roman subway to walking, which is a small enough matter. But sell it to enough morally outraged revolutionaries and you will surely increase the general crowdedness of the world and shrink the memorial lists of their victims.

In spite of the determined cleansing operations and the effectiveness of such contraceptives as Depro-Provera, populations appear to be increasing everywhere and, given the human capacity for balkanization, so are the language barriers. This is bad news for travelers since the gabble of a foreign language can surround the most elemental transactions with an aura of incipient chaos. Having made the mistake of arriving in Rome during the week of Opus Dei's celebration of the beatification of its founder, Escriva de Belaguer, we must settle for a third-rate pensione and have to communicate with the manager by sign language so that the crowd effect of the city itself is not momentarily escaped from but intensified. No foreign place can be as unorganized as it seems to one who cannot understand the language. This is why travel can help you understand the utopian promise of the Pentecost experience. Here as the Apostles were gathered together, tongues of fire appeared, settled on each of them, and they were filled with the Holy Spirit. Thus inspired, they spoke to a crowd of "devout Jews of every nation under heaven" and a linguistic community was instantly created since each foreigner heard the speakers in his or her own language.

Our text for this marvelous event is the *The Acts of the Apostles,* Chapter 2. If the deconstructionist Jacques Derrida had been present he might have been one of those who suspected that the speakers were drunk from too much new wine. But the text itself is easily enough deconstructed now in favor of a subversive between-the-lines meaning that adumbrates a secular Pentecost for a gnostic elite. The latter knows all too well what lives in and thrives by a crowd-bedeviled culture drunk on its constitutive and unstable texts. In Florence I read that, in spite of considerable opposition, Cambridge University had awarded Derrida an honorary doctorate of letters. Would those who objected to the award have agreed with St. Peter's common-sense rebuttal of the deconstructive skeptics: it was too early in the day to reduce the Pentecost experience to drunkenness?

Perhaps deconstructionists should be seen as travelers trying to be at home in a world from which they have been alienated by textually misled crowds. Being alien, they must like all travelers accept the burden of translation. When you travel you are alien in proportion as you cannot translate into your own terms the otherness of mentalities, languages, and of course money. Pounds, francs, marks, and lira are the communal expression of particular places that in the interest of their own integrity cannot help but be alienating. For a traveler, a strange currency symbolizes the crowdedness of the world as much as a strange language does. "Put money in thy purse," says Iago to the gullible Roderigo in *Othello*, as if with money he could go securely and unalienated anywhere. Marx in the *Economic and Philosophic Manuscripts* thinks otherwise: "the *divine power* of money...resides in its *essence* as the alienated and exteriorized species-life of man." Travelers who must, in the course of a few weeks, cross several European borders know that he has a point. In the Marxist dispensation of a secular Pentecost, they would be relieved of the burden of monetary translation, and might even be led to believe that in due time a worldwide linguistic community, impervious to Derrida and his kind, might follow. In the meantime, with Iago's advice in mind, they had best put money in their purses, keep their phrase books handy, and not be surprised when they have to pay five thousand lira, as we did in Rome, for a not very warm shower.

Money, to give it its due, has always meant protection from crowds. No one knows this better than those who travel on a shoestring. Rich Americans are less likely to feel alienated abroad because they stay in posh English-speaking places and ride about in cabs or rented limousines. For better or worse, the wealthy have always been able to use their castles or mansions as isolation from crowds. Versailles, as we learned one Sunday, can be a very crowded place, but for Louis XVI, thanks to the divine power of money, it was a refined form of crowd-evasion. In the end the crowd won, however: in October of 1789 that band of women marched out from Paris shouting, "Bread, bread!" So the King and his family were driven back to Paris, where in due time he was delivered over to that merciless social-equalizer and crowd-exciter, the guillotine. But the Versailles impulse dies hard. Now in the Western democracies those who can afford to are emigrating to suburbs and exurbs to avoid the crowded and often bread-hungry inner cities—precisely where the not especially affluent middle-class traveler is likely to spend most of his time.

A great deal of our fear of the crowded and technologically complex city can be traced to the romantic impulse, whether its provenance is American or European. The romantics, as Harold Bloom contends in *The American Religion*, were committed to a gnostic cult of the inner self and the imagination. For people like Thoreau,

Emerson, Wordsworth, Shelley, and Keats, the big city is the supreme artifact of the Demiurge, the anti-God, who opposes the true religion of the self. In the Bloomean sense, the true God is more likely to be symbolized by Thoreau's loon, Shelley's skylark, Wordsworth's daffodils, or Keats's nightingale. In Keats's sonnet "To One Who Has Been Long in City Pent," the poet returning from the city finds it "very sweet to look into the fair/ And open face of heaven" and breathe a prayer of thanksgiving, which makes it clear enough that hell is exactly where a romantic and nature-loving environmentalist like Bill McKibben thinks it is. Sadly, however, Keats spent his last days pent up in an apartment in Rome that overlooks the Spanish Steps where no nightingales sang, though now often enough there is technologically amplified rock music.

Thanks perhaps to Opus Dei, the Steps were crowded and noisy the week of our visit, but so was everything else in Rome. On Sunday an estimated 200,000 crowded into St. Peter's Square for the beatification. Coming in late, we saw parts of the celebration on a badly focused television screen and had to depend on our son, who had come early with his binoculars, for a deferred account. We were glad to see the security measures in operation, remembering that two days before our previous visit the Pope had been shot here in far less crowded circumstances. Obviously, the Opus Dei people were not worried about security; for them the beatification had the safety of a triumphant communal experience.

Not all Catholics, including some in the Vatican itself, seem to have been so jubilant. Opus Dei was too secretive and authoritarian for some, too inclined to bypass the Church's chain of command for others. There was a suspicion of pro-fascist sympathies in its Spanish beginnings, and no doubt there were those who suspected a gnostic taint in its clandestine world-abjuring spirituality, though Harold Bloom might have had a hard time seeing in it a romantic-gnostic cult of the true inner self. In the afternoon of the beatification, a line of people three or four wide and a mile long filed by the tomb of the founder. Inner selves don't huddle together this way; like Wordsworth, they are more inclined to "wander lonely as a cloud," communing with the "golden daffodils."

In any event, the Opus Dei people were too respectful in their togetherness to be a mob. Two days before, as we stood in line to get into the Sistine Chapel, someone behind us complained, "What a mob!" Inside the chapel there was no mob, only a well-mannered audience whose admiration of the wonderfully reclaimed ceiling made it an esthetic community. A mob is what happens to a crowd when some event activates its potential synergy for destructive purposes. Two millennia ago, not far from what is today St. Peter's Square, Shakespeare's Mark Antony skillfully exploited the assassination of Julius Caesar as he turned a confused crowd of plebeians into a rampaging mob directed against Brutus and his fellow conspirators.

What we fear most about a mob is the all-consuming self-transcending experience we sense its aroused members are having, and in that fear is also a sense of how limited is the casual onlooker's ability to resist the mob's invitation to a communal life abundant. The precipitating event may be perceived victimization, as in the later Los Angeles riots, or conversely a fan-exalting basketball victory in Chicago, in which one might see a vengeful and celebrational thrashing of those forces or agencies that could have resulted in the victimization of defeat. With some British soccer fans, apparently, winning or losing is less important as an inciter to mob-like conduct than the inability of potential hoodlums to defend themselves against the intoxication of the game itself. And then there was the shooting of a German officer in Paris in November of 1938 that precipitated throughout Germany those hoodlum attacks on the Jews that we know as Crystal Night—when respectable middle-class citizens behaved like rampaging rock-music fans.

The thing, in any event, is the transcendence; you can be lost and bored in a crowd but never in a mob. A mob tends to experience an esthetic unity of destruction and creation. Shakespeare's aroused plebeians speak prose, but their actions are a violent kind of poetry—the poetry to which they have been inspired by Mark Antony's superb blank verse. We see the same esthetic at work in Leni Riefenstahl's prize-winning *Triumph of the Will* in which Hitler, reprising Mark Antony at the 1934 Party Day festival at Nuremberg, molded a crowd of 200,000 into a community whose hoodlum potential put it for a terrible time beyond the grace of any Pentecost.

No doubt there are those who would have felt as threatened among the 200,000 at St. Peter's Square as they would have among the 200,000 at Nuremberg. Whether or not we are Bloomean gnostics, the terrible events of our century have made it easy to believe that the integrity of the self demands distance from crowds, and never more than when they disguise themselves as communities. For such beleaguered selves even the most benevolent-seeming communities lust after authentic inner selves the way those women marching to Versailles lusted after the selfish autonomy of the King. And communities always want more than bread. This is why for some of us the texts that determine the language of communities must be deconstructed, even at the risk of casting doubt on the reality and durability of the poetry-creating inner self, and on the deconstructionist as well. Keats, dying by the Spanish Steps far from the nightingales and without the conventional communal attachments that deny death its dominion, seems to have been tormented by this doubt.

Many of us have to combine this doubt with a foot-dragging commitment to the secular and sacred institutions that try to structure both our world and our lives. But the institutions realize themselves as communities that in a liberal democracy are often so hard to distinguish from self-threatening crowds that the refusal to make the distinction becomes itself a virtue, especially given the ease with which narcissistic selves pass for the gnostic variety. One result is the disgust with crowd-fostering democracy felt by many who gathered at Nuremberg to be touched by the magic of the Füehrer and incorporated through his enhanced selfhood into a more abundant life.

Population-reducers like Hitler and Stalin envisioned the world in terms of ever larger redeemed communities from which dissenting selves would be eliminated. This was a profane variation on that other redemption story that Michelangelo so laboriously described on the Sistine ceiling, where God's extended finger, almost touching Adam's, invites him and his progeny to life abundant. But such variations are without end in a congested and balkanized world. So there are those who share the New Age hope for a world community that animates the handful of specialists at work, busy as bees, in Biosphere II in the Arizona desert. And according to some diehard optimists, the new Euro Disneyland outside Paris signals a paradigm shift of attention that will counter the centrifugal forces of our world with a carnivalesque esthetic superior to Leni Riefenstahl's at Nuremberg—a hope perhaps that looks forward to a deconstructed Sistine ceiling in which God is discovered to have all along been Mickey Mouse.

Not having visited Euro Disneyland, but home again and jetlagged among familiar and benevolent crowds, we discovered that the media were still trying to come to grips with the Los Angeles disaster. I learned from *Rolling Stone* that the riots had in effect been predicted by rap musicians like Ice-T and L. L. Cool. Rap, writes Alan Light, is a music that not only "makes listeners laugh and dance and sing along" but also "makes its audience think and tells the truth about its world." So in the esthetic of rap music too there may be a hope, not simply for the hip-hop generation but for the lot of us, that creation will follow destruction and alienated crowds will be translated into loving communities.

Whether or not this is good news for gnostic inner selves is another matter. In any event, and *pace* Hassan II, it implies a characteristic American conviction that, if in politics or anything else you can only choose between bad and worse, you really have no choice at all.

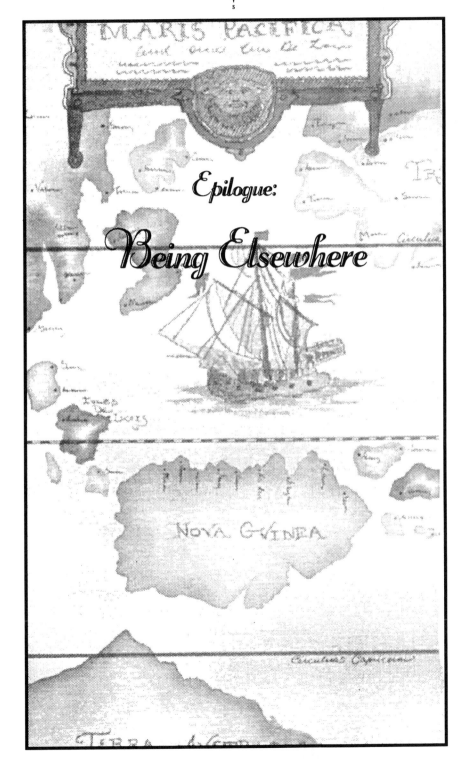

Epilogue:
Being Elsewhere

ᐯeing ℰlsewhere
1951-1982

n a family, nothing is more surprising and life-renewing than the return in a new context of an event thought at first to be singular. In their cumulative effect, such returns reach mysteriously both ahead and back in time so that, however particular the time and place of an event, one may be both elsewhere and at home. But all this must be proven on one's pulse as one begins the risky, repetitive, continually surprising, and always mysterious enterprise of family living. And so in due time I am trying desperately to finish a book review as my wife's vital contractions accelerate. Suddenly it is time, she hurries to the kitchen sink to shampoo her hair, I stop in mid-paragraph and hurry her to the hospital where soon our second daughter is born.

Without the omniscience of the plot-controlling novelist, I am unable to foresee that many years later the daughter will be with us in Paris. She will rise early in our Left Bank bed-and-breakfast quarters to go running, and I will lie there with the joyous picture of her taking her favorite route: up rue Bonaparte to the Seine, down to Pont St. Michel and across it to circle Notre Dame, over to the Right Bank and down to the Louvre, then home by way of Pont Royal. In the time constraints of the family plot, however, I can only flashback to our honeymoon in the conventional lakeside cottage—where, because of primitive accommodations, my bride must wash her beautiful hair in the lake and I am able to watch her from a cabin window as she kneels on the edge of the dock. But both shampooings are preparing me to think badly of the man we will ultimately meet in St. Peter's Square in Rome two days after the Pope has been shot, we being there in part for a family reason: to stand on the roof of the basilica and take pictures from the same spot where our grand-touring first daughter once stood. The man is with his wife and he is still angry. They had come down from Germany the day before the historic event and the wife, overdue for a shampoo and hairdo, made an appointment with a hair-dresser, so that they arrived in the square an hour too late for the shooting. My sympathies are with the wife, who looks nice, if somewhat chastened, with her fresh hairdo. Hadn't she only wanted to look nice for her husband, and perhaps for the Pope as well—just as my shampooing wife had wanted to look nice for me?

Repetitions in good novels are incremental just as they are in medieval ballads, where the repetition of verses in changing contexts carries the plot ahead. Thus in *The Great Gatsby* ,the repetition of moments that articulate a discovery of illusion after glorious expectation build up incrementally to that final moment when the reader is elsewhere with those long-ago Dutch sailors who in a "transitory enchanted moment" behold the "fresh, green breast of the new world," never dreaming how far it will fall short of its promise. But the plot of a family, too, is structured with the incremental repetitions of secular and sacred rituals that dramatize the unspoken conviction that the failure to celebrate a recurring event is an implicit judgment that it was worthless to begin with. In vital families the celebration of each baptism and birthday is separate and special and yet has been enrichingly prepared for by the celebration of all previous baptisms and birthdays. The eggs are colored each Easter Eve in the same basement room at the same time, but the children, like developing writers, refine their techniques and come up with novel effects. And each family has its own ritual style, its own way of vitalizing its identifying plot. Families that have lost, or never had, the capacity for plot-sustaining innovations are condemned like the victims of autism to repetition without increment, which is the fate of those lost souls who people Dante's *Inferno*. Even apparently disastrous interruptions of the familiar ritual pattern may, as in novels, turn out to be memorable surprises. Thus on the eve of a Sunday confirmation, the car breaks down and we must hire two taxis to get everyone to the church and back for the celebratory breakfast afterward. The children, excited with their first taxi ride, obviously think that the failure of the family car has made their day.

The family picnic, like Christmas one of the most incrementally repetitious of rituals, is one of the best ways to be at once elsewhere and home, which is why the better the picnic, the more everyone enjoys being home again. So after the children have gone off to establish their own separate yet interconnected lives, the picnic *à deux* continues to be a family affair. We are, for instance, at Versailles in mid-May, early picnic time at home. We buy ham sandwiches and cans of Coke at a stand near the Fountain of Latina and go down where the white blossoms of the great chestnut trees are tossing like pompoms in the light midday wind. As we eat we can see a corner of the Petit Trianon where the randy Louis XV had once enjoyed the favors of Madame Du Barry, doomed many years later to die on the guillotine. There is a tree-nestled honeymoon privacy about the place that takes me back to the much less opulent privacy of our own honeymoon cabin in the pines. The latter becomes the destination of a family picnic, the aim being to show the children their true beginnings and at the same time grill hamburgers on a new charcoal burner. The children are respectful enough but hardly overwhelmed. Like the readers of *The Great Gatsby* who encounter for the first time the valley of ashes between West Egg and Manhattan, they must take it on faith that the place will ultimately prove to be a significant elsewhere in the family plot. Later, on the beach, they are more impressed with the improvement of hot hamburgers over previous picnic fare.

But for my wife and me it is a Proustian return, and I remember our long honeymoon walk on a golden August afternoon, down the narrow dirt road that runs past the cabin and out into pastoral farmland. We are living for the moment, dispensed from historical time like Fitzgerald's Dutch sailors, not knowing that the walk is prologue to an incremental repetition of elsewhere walks. Thus we are at Giverny in France on another golden afternoon in order to see Claude Monet's watery pastoral domain. It is easy to imagine the artist at work in his studio there, smoking his daily forty cigarettes in the domestic silence he insisted on,. But there is little sense of family left, though as modern painters go he was, like his friend Matisse, a better than average family man. When we have had our fill of his water lilies and Japanese prints, we walk down a country road that Monet would have known well, but we are no longer thinking of him. He has said of his work: "The subject is of secondary importance to me; what I want to reproduce is what exists between the subject and me." He has become of secondary importance to us. What we will reproduce later is not Monet but the repeated timelessness of that walk on a pastoral afternoon.

Or we are at Kildare in Ireland, walking down a fairy-story country lane through hay-sweet horse fields, having no other objective after the exciting noise of Paris, London, and Dublin than living for an hour or two in a dispensation of green silence. We come to the bone-white remnant of a castle, stoop to enter its trash-littered keep. It is open like a giant chimney so that we can see birds wheeling far above us in the silver satin sky, and we know that if our sons were with us they would find some way to climb up there and scare us to death. Or we are in Venice, having left St. Mark's and crossed the Grand Canal by the Rialto bridge to go honeymoon walking by narrow winding ways and across murky and rotten-smelling small canals till we are pleasantly lost—unlike that doomed bachelor Gustave Aschenbach, who, after a similar excursion in pursuit of his beloved Tadzio in Thomas Mann's *Death in Venice*, ends up miserably distraught. We come to a small café where we get excellent white wine and sit outside drinking it, a stone's throw from a soccer-loud schoolyard. The players are caught up like honeymooners in their mysterious elsewhere, and they send me synchronically back to another schoolyard, to which I have been called because our eldest son has been injured in a pickup football game during afternoon recess. I must return him, fortunately not for long, to the hospital where he was born.

In the developing family plot there are no elsewheres of pure escape, just as in Melville's great novel there is no place where Moby Dick is not present. So we are in New York, returning along Fifty-fifth Street after a visit to the U. N., and note that something is happening at the Third Avenue intersection. A man in a drab black suit hurries past us, extracting something from a pocket of his jacket. It is a purple stole. At the intersection two police cars have halted the impatiently honking traffic, a city bus has pulled up at an odd angle, someone covered by a yellow tarp is lying beside it and the priest is there reading from a small black book. A bystander tells us that the victim was a young bicycle rider whose head had been crushed by a wheel of the bus. The corner of the tarp keeps flapping up and the stalled traffic keeps on honking. There is nothing to do but walk on, carrying the image of our second son lying on a curb beside stalled traffic. I have been summoned from home by one of the other children. He lies there quiet as death, his face drained of color. He had been riding his bike on the wrong side of the street, crashed head-on into an auto, and ended up sprawled on the hood. The bike is a twisted ruin. As I bend over him, his eyes open. An ambulance arrives and again it is off to the hospital, by now the most familiar of elsewheres.

I will soon learn that he is only badly shaken up—but as I await the verdict, I am sitting in the same room I had occupied a year before as I waited to learn whether our third son had broken his arm. He has fallen from the kitchen countertop in the process of trying to steal cookies from an upper cupboard and I have been called off the golf course to rush him to the hospital. So in the family plot, incremental repetitions can go backward as well as forward in that suspension of chronological sequence that Forster so admires in novels. Members of families have always known this, at least existentially. Once novelists learned to imitate the experience of time in families, novels have never been the same.

This fact, however, has not kept modern novelists (to say nothing of counterculture gurus like the British psychiatrist R. D. Laing) from doing their part to publicize the family as an institution uncongenial to artistic personalities. A proper place to remember this bias is in Forster's own Bloomsbury, an area that, thanks to the British Museum, the fine periodicals library of the University of London, and the Safeway supermarket, has always been one of the most agreeable of elsewheres for us. Bloomsbury, like all bohemias and countercultures, was an aesthetic enclave in which creativity and self-enhancement, not family nurturing, came first. From the perspective of such places, the more ideal or happy the family, the more its plot is a prison from which the creative individual must escape. This may be why family members like Hemingway or Joyce, who are scheduled to become novelists, act as though they need to justify their escape by making their families more unhappy than they might otherwise have been. Perhaps they are motivated by an anticipatory fear that if a family could be as successfully plotted as a novel, it could not help being anti-novel. Most likely this fear was behind what his biographer P. N. Furbank called Forster's distrust of marriage as an institution and his irritation "at having to write 'marriage fiction.'" Only the work of art is supposed to be happy without crippling dependence on elsewheres outside itself. The happy family is its adversary, which may be why novelists and other artists tend to make such a mess of things when they get in a family way themselves.

But it would probably be better to speak of good rather than happy families: "happy" suggests an invulnerability to the happenstance of time. Good families are sometimes less than happy just as good novels are at some points less than good. Certainly there were moments when the Tolstoy family, thanks to the master's passionate eccentricities, was unhappy in its own way. Good families can survive the same vicissitudes that make other families bad. Like good novels they depend on the strength of their commitment to well-chosen plots. Perhaps nothing is more likely to make a potentially good family unhappy and bad than the mistake of putting happiness first, as Tolstoy's *Anna Karenina* and Flaubert's *Madame Bovary* do. The analogous mistake for the novelist is his failure as he writes to keep out of his mind the need to so overwhelm his readers and critics that his self-doubts will be gone forever. In our culture, unfortunately, families, like individuals, can become so addicted to happiness that anything short of continual domestic euphoria is intolerable. Perhaps, then, families should be graded less by their degree of happiness than by their ability to stand up to the causes of unhappiness. Indeed, one of the functions of a good family plot is to teach the liberating lesson that it is possible to live purposefully, and even fulfillingly, without being always happy. A condition of uninterrupted happiness, in fact, would mean repetition without increment, and without mystery or surprise. Not having had a chance to learn this, Anna Karenina and Madame Bovary have no alternative but to sacrifice themselves to the well-being of their novels.

If a family can do without unalloyed happiness, it cannot do without the renewing power of those returns from elsewhere that celebrate its always mysterious and surprising existence in time. So we are at the airport awaiting our third daughter's return from a year's schooling in Florence. After she arrives, I am distracted for a moment, then turn to see that all three daughters have joined hands and are celebrating their reunion with a joyful dance. A few years later my wife and I are elsewhere again, in Florence now, visiting the room in the pensione where that daughter lived during her great year abroad, and again I see my daughters dancing on the carpet of the concourse. In my mind they will never stop dancing.

John P. Sisk, a native of Spokane, was educated at Gonzaga University and the University of Washington. He has been a member of the English Department Faculty at Gonzaga University since 1938, teaching Shakespeare, American Literature, and English Romanticism. He served in the U. S. Air Force in World War II and was discharged in 1946 as a captain.

He was a Senior Fellow of the National Endowment for the Humanities in 1972-73 and has served as a consultant and panelist for the Aspen Institute program on Communications and Society (1974, 1975); National Endowment for the Humanities (1975-79, 1982); and the National Humanities Center (1980, 1981). He is an Associate of the National Faculty and Arnold Professor of the Humanities (Emeritus) at Gonzaga, where he also holds the position of Scholar-in-Residence.

His critical essays, short fiction, and reviews have appeared in the nation's most important periodicals since 1949, most recently in *The American Scholar, First Things, The Georgia Review, The Hudson Review, America,* and *Salmagundi.* These have been collected in two previous works, *Person and Institution* (Notre Dame University, Fides Press, 1970) and *The Tyrannies of Virtue* (University of Oklahoma Press, 1990). A *Trial of Strength* won the Carl Foreman Award for best short novel in an international competition sponsored by Harcourt, Brace; Highroads Productions; and Collins (England) in 1961.

He lives in Spokane with his wife Gwen—when they are not traveling.